For My Space Man.

Enjoy!

DEATH DOESN'T VACATION ON OKALOOSA ISLAND

GEORGE D. KING

George W King

authorHOUSE®

AuthorHouse™
1663 Liberty Drive
Bloomington, IN 47403
www.authorhouse.com
Phone: 1 (800) 839-8640

Published by AuthorHouse 05/23/2016

ISBN: 978-1-5246-1009-8 (sc)
ISBN: 978-1-5246-1041-8 (e)

Print information available on the last page.

This book is printed on acid-free paper.

...to the one who took care of me and my siblings when there was no one else to do it.

Visit **Death Doesn't Vacation on Okaloosa Island** on **Face Book** to get updates, a picture of the setting, and read about the sequel**, Treachery on Okaloosa Island.**

The characters in this novel are totally fictional--made-up from my imagination. I have known so many people during my life, especially students, but I certainly do not intend my fictional ones to resemble any real people. Much of the setting of the novel will be recognized by some readers, but many places have been altered and many places have been added where they do not exist in reality. As far as I know, none of the happenings of this work of fiction have ever occurred on the Panhandle of Florida.

Okaloosa – Choctaw Indian
Oka (water) – Lusa (black)

1

The La Mancha

Max found her body when he came to work this morning. I heard later he told the deputies he found her at about 8:10, but I know that's not so and I wonder why he picked that particular time and why the lie?

Like many of the people who work on Okaloosa Island, Max lives somewhere off of Highway 98, The Miracle Strip, as we call it. During the year over four million people visit the Emerald Coast on the Panhandle of Florida for their vacations and traffic on 98 is horrendous during the summer months when school is out as families come to fill the thousands of condos along the white sandy beaches. During the fall and winter almost as many hearty Snow Birds fill the same condos for weeks at a time. Those of us who live here usually welcome our visitors with genuine Southern hospitality.

If you could persuade Brantley to fly you from Pensacola to Destin along 98 in his Sikorsky helicopter, you would leave the barren sands of the Air Command as you approach the Island, see Fort Walton Beach out the window on the left across the Sound and straight ahead of you the six stark white buildings of the La Mancha complex with their brick-red roofs. As you fly over Santa Rosa Blvd that splits the Island in half, you realize the Island is only a few hundred yards wide at its widest point.

About three miles later Brooks Bridge juts out over the Sound from the north connecting the Island to the mainland. You would probably see Brantley glance down to his left to see Launie's place where he secretly visits. For the next six miles the enormous Choctawhatchee Bay is on the left, Highway 98 winds down the middle of the remainder of the Island which appears to be uninhabited but has some military installations and several pull-offs where people can walk to the beach, and then you would

3

fly over the cut, The Destin Pass Bridge, where the Bay is connected to the beautiful dark emerald green Gulf of Mexico.

Santa Rosa Blvd, a flat smooth almost straight four lane street, is a right turn at the stop light at the foot of Brooks Bridge as you leave Fort Walton Beach going east toward Destin. It separates the Gulf side of the Island from the almost black water of the Santa Rosa Waterway, or the Sound, as we call it. That side of the Island has apartment complexes and beautiful single family homes, many valued at a million or more. The Gulf side is a three mile strip of condo complexes which bring in more tax monies than anything in Okaloosa County.

At the west end of the public access of the Blvd, the concrete barriers to the Air Command stop the public traffic. Just before reaching there, you make a sharp left turn into the La Mancha complex which is the last of the many condo complexes. The La Mancha has six buildings all named for common things around the Gulf with a large painting of whatever it is called on its end. The paintings are about as old as the complex and have been preserved from the salty air with coat upon coat of clear shellac. Bicycle Bob told me a lot of money was paid to a well-known local artist to design and paint them.

The La Mancha is the oldest of the condo complexes, over forty years old, but very desirable to those many tourists who come to lie on the warm white sands every summer because of its sprawling beach. Hundreds of Snow Birds return year after year because they like its seclusion. A low thick rock wall surrounds the whole complex; it looks like the top of an old-world castle, crenulated because of the sturdy pillars positioned every fifteen feet or so that are taller than the wall. The wall is painted the same bright white as the buildings which causes a sharp contrast to the almost six acres of beautiful green grassy lawns. Hundreds of palms dot the lawns where they have been planted and tropical flowers bloom around their trunks all summer.

A high ugly chain link fence runs across the west end of the property dividing the La Mancha from the Air Command where there is nothing but barren sand spotted with a new growth of struggling pine trees and scrub growth as far as you can see. The fence is in serious disrepair with jagged pieces sticking out in the air and ominous holes with twisted broken pieces of wire left gaping through the years. If the La Mancha was not such a happy place for vacationing the fence could create a spooky presence.

When I moved here, Bicycle Bob told me that the Sand Dollar building stood on the site many years before the other five buildings were built; that it had been a saloon and relaxation place for the airmen—a strip joint. Bob gave me that huge smile and boisterous laugh of his, and I took that to mean it was a house of ill repute. It's the business end of the complex now with the rental offices in front just after you enter the security gate to the property and the Marvin's maintenance offices in the back. Bette's office is on the second floor, the top floor, facing the entrance.

Many of the units of the La Mancha are owned by people in nearby states so many of the 310 condos are occupied with them and the rest are filled with summer visitors this beautiful June morning. The happy sounds of children playing on the beach and splashing in the water will soon fill the air as the sun rises over the horizon over at Destin to shimmer on the water of the Gulf.

Like I said, Max was not being truthful when he talked to the sheriff's deputies when they arrived. I know because I had just made coffee and heard him arrive. He drives a classic '56 Ford Fairlane coupe which has glass packs that he and his dad installed and everybody in the complex hears them when he turns in at the La Mancha gate from Santa Rosa Blvd. I was out on my balcony with a cup of Folgers when he came along the walk around the corner of the Pelican, my building. He waved at me, walked down the boardwalk past the gazebo, unlocked the big box which holds the beach umbrellas and chairs, and started carrying them out onto the sand.

Max is a very good looking young man and he knows it; the girls on the beach always seem to flock close to where he sits under an umbrella each day after he finishes putting up the umbrellas and chairs. His blue-green eyes mimic the color of the Gulf and his short cropped black hair is a big contrast to his deep brown tan. His physique would make Apollo blush.

He's 'vertically challenged,' he says, but the kid is built. Those folding beach chairs weigh over ten pounds apiece and Max has developed a routine where he hooks them together around his body and lifts up eight of them at a time. He carries them out across the sand—sometimes almost running— and sits them out in pairs.

Then he lines up the big blue umbrellas, takes his drill with a special sand auger attached and drills down so he can sink the umbrella poles deep into the sand; they look like blue mushrooms in my imagination.

But Max didn't get here by 8:10 as he told Detective Emile Morat of the Okaloosa County Sheriff's Department later this morning. And I wonder why he claimed to be here?

2

Much Earlier that Morning

I retired from almost forty years of teaching English to high school seniors and came to the beach on the Gulf from Albuquerque where I found my condo on the third floor of the Pelican at the La Mancha. It's about as close to paradise as I can imagine. There's something magical about walking out onto my balcony to see the ever changing waters of the Gulf, the magnificent sunrises, and the equally awesome sunsets.

The area is called the Emerald Coast because the waters really are emerald colored ninety percent of the time. When we get a storm, the water rages and turns a nasty dark grey—and it can be very frightening. We don't have many storms in June, but we did last week. Somewhere in the depths of the waters great strings of seaweed were ripped apart and as the waves pushed them into the shore they began to fill the shallows. The storm changed the beach line and created a bank which hides whatever is below it from view even if you are standing on the beach a few yards away.

As a teacher of literature, I have read many books about the sea, but I never quite comprehended what a glassy sea was. The last two or three days the Gulf has been so quite that indeed it was a mirror. Yesterday, a huge vertical cloud was out on the horizon and its shadow was reflected clear into the beach below the gazebo. The Gulf was flat and the waves, if you could call them that, just barely lapped at the beach, but that storm out there somewhere had changed everything this morning as the waves were rolling in.

I walked very early this morning. As I headed west along the sand in the shadowy dawn, I made out the outline of the seagull I have named Jonathan L. He's sitting on the volleyball net pole all by himself as he does for hours at a time, and then he will soar into the sky so far up I can hardly see him—all alone. At least, I imagine that it is the same bird I see sitting there on the pole so much.

As I said, this morning the waves have returned and occasionally one slaps the shore with a loud pop—almost the sound of a gunshot.

Ivan had done a number on our beach when the huge hurricane slammed onto land in 2004. The dunes of sand held in place by sea oats and the low growing, but clinging beach morning glory and other plants were all whipped away in a swirl of huge treacherous waves. It would take years for the bitter switch grass and marsh hay cord grass to gain footholds again. Many of us had spent hours planting sea oats and other native plants in the manmade dunes which were dozed up to protect the La Mancha.

The stand of thirty to forty foot high pines which covered the Air Command property on our west end went smashing into the Sound and hit the high bank on the other side where Fort Walton Beach seems to perch. Some of the debris piled up so high that the streets of the town were filled several feet deep and it took days to clear it away. Boats of all sorts crashed in the high bank and were tossed on 98 shutting down traffic for days. The Sound had to be dredged from Navarre, the little town eleven miles to our west, to the mouth of Choctawhatchee Bay which is the enormous bay of water which goes all the way down past the Pass at Destin. Fort Walton Beach Landing was destroyed to never be built back as it was. Ivan had done a real number on the area.

The Dolphin building at the La Mancha had taken the biggest hit from Ivan. It's across the pool from my building. The two of them, the Pelican and the Dolphin, form a V shape on either side of our big pool facing the Gulf. Two or three condos on the west end of the two bottom floors of the Dolphin were ripped off by Ivan. A palm tree snapped in two and rammed through the sliding glass doors of Condo 10 along with five or six feet of sand. A huge sink hole appeared under the end of the building where two propane tanks had been years ago. The west boardwalk to the beach was totally demolished and landed in a pile of rubble far into the Air Command land.

Before it plowed into us, we couldn't see past the grove of pines into the Air Command part of the Island, but now the land is bare as far as you can see except for the new little pines and vines which seem to have magically appeared in the sand. The Command hadn't built anything close to the point where the public access ends, so the mystery of what the area is used for remains a mystery. Walking along the beach past the warning sign doesn't allow us to see what is in there either since nothing is built on the beach side.

I walked past that faded red warning sign which says, CLOSED AREA, and underneath that it says something about a clearance needed but we don't pay attention to it. We don't think it means the beach even though the sign is not far from the water. I walk past it every day as do hundreds of vacationers, and I have never seen anyone stopped or anyone who might be stationed to stop people.

This morning as I turn back east from there toward the morning sun which is peeking over the Destin horizon, a wave pops really loud and I am momentarily startled. I guess I actually jump a little, but I quickly cover my embarrassment as I see someone hurrying west toward me—almost running. He is looking back over his shoulder and when he turns and sees me, he abruptly stops.

"Good morning, Marvin."

He is out of breath and mutters, "Mornin."

"You're out very early?"

"Yeah, had to fix a pipe, and then decided to run a little."

"I don't think I have ever seen you on the beach."

9

"Oh yeah, I come down here a lot."

Why was he being so defensive and I'm certain I had never seen him down here this early before.

The people in the complex are calling me 'Prof, the Snoop' behind my back, I hear. It's true I see a lot, and after teaching all those teenagers for years, I pay attention to what is going on around me. I had students who thought I had the 'proverbial eye in the back of my head.'

"Hey, I gotta go!" Marvin hollers as he starts running on west toward the Command property.

I walk on east as the sun is now fully up over the horizon of the Gulf on the other side of Destin six miles away. The buildings in the distance are silhouetted against the sky which is full of big puffy clouds all tinted bright orange around their upper edges. What a beautiful sunrise.

I turned to look back west and Marvin was nowhere to be seen. How in the world had he disappeared, I wondered?

I was nearly even with the gazebo when Jonathan L flew straight up and let out a shriek-squawk, and a voice said, "You're out early."

As I turn rather startled, I am face to face, I really mean, face to brim, with Brantley.

Everyone at the La Mancha knows Brantley. He is rather slight of build, but very muscular. His slim body is hard with muscles that are really defined. He is totally strange too, about as strange as that name his mother most likely found in some romance novel when he was born. Every morning he comes out the sliding door of his first floor condo in the Dolphin and starts picking up any trash left by inconsiderate people. He also cleans out the outdoor bar-b-q grills.

However, he wears a genuine Indian Safari Pith Helmet which he calls a sola topee, and very short and skimpy black Speedos. He paints the helmet a different theme every few days and this morning it is harlequin with purple and yellow diamonds painted all around the brim. A court jester! A children's clown!

We hear his mother used to make him clean up around the complex when he did something she thought needed to be punished, but we haven't seen his mother for some time. Yet, he continues the same routine every morning when he's at La Mancha.

I seldom see him on the beach, but he is frequently standing watching me from the gazebo. This morning he is right down next to the water and perhaps I imagine it but he seems stranger than usual. He keeps looking around like he lost something. But maybe he is just looking for debris.

I said, "Yes, but I usually walk this early. You're the one who is out early today. Besides, you never get on the sand."

I noticed his right hand was heavily wrapped in a bandage, "Have you hurt yourself?"

"Yeah, cut it on a piece of broken glass in one of the bar-b-q grills. Sliced it right between my finger and thumb. It's nothing."

He glanced around and replied, "Seen anything unusual? Uh, you know, stuff the surf might have washed up on the beach from last week's storm?"

I thought…just you in that outlandish helmet…but I said, "No, the sun still came up and the waves are still rolling into the shore."

He didn't respond nor think I was clever I guess, but wheeled around and ran along the beach to the west end of the property and up the steps of the boardwalk there and disappeared around the front of his building. What a strange guy!

I really don't know him, but I hear he lives in the condo which belongs to his mom and she often kicks him out for some reason and then he begs his way back in, but we haven't seen her for at least two or three years. He told one of his neighbors she had moved back up to Memphis to be close to her sister.

He has a collection of Japanese weapons inherited from an uncle who got them back into the country from his tour of the Pacific. Bicycle Bob told me he was in Brantley's condo once and that Brantley has them hanging in a collection on his bedroom wall.

Brantley is a corporate pilot for some oil company and is gone for days at a time.

I read an article in the *NorthWest Daily* about how he saved fourteen men who were stranded on a rig in a tropical storm. He had flown back and forth from Mobile five times in winds as high as 60 mph to pick them off a rig. The winds had blown his helicopter off course twice but somehow Brantley had realized he was off course and had straightened out the copter and found the rig.

As he was getting one load of men off the rig, a gust of wind blew the copter very close to one of the pilings and one of the sled shoes grazed it. He was within twenty feet of the water when he rectified the Sikorsky. The article quoted a company official as saying Brantley becomes a superman when he is at the controls of the bright yellow Sikorsky helicopter. He had made five trips because the copter only hauls three passengers and one of them had to sit next to him in the cockpit.

The children of the men wrote him letters thanking him for saving their dads. He still has the letters displayed on the ceiling of the plane above his pilot seat. He shows them to everyone who rides with him.

Brantley has been with the company for several years and has earned many bonuses flying company personal out to the rigs in the Gulf so I guess he's not entirely weird as I think he is, and without a doubt he has a big heart.

3
About 8:30

Jonathan L landed on the volleyball net pole as I climbed the ramp up to the gazebo. He seemed agitated about something as he just barely landed when he flew away again. I walked down the boardwalk and walked the sidewalk around the end of my building, took the elevator to the third floor, entered my condo, turned on the Cuisinart coffee maker, and headed for the shower.

When I got out and dressed, I walked into the kitchen where the smell of Folgers filled the air. I filled my big orange Winnie the Pooh cup which the grandkids brought me from Disney World, added the half-and-half, and slid the door open to the balcony.

Jonathan swooped in onto the pole gulping down something that was much too big to swallow at one time. The seagulls ('Swine Birds' as Peter Sellers would say) were swarming around something down on the water's edge a hundred yards or so from the gazebo. The recent storms had created that bank at the water's edge that I couldn't see over from my vantage point. Jonathan quickly joined them. Probably a dead Pompano, I thought. They would dive down, go straight up, let out that shriek-squawk that so identifies them, hover, and dive again. Must be something big for there were at least two dozen of them.

Marvin certainly seemed unusual this morning, I thought. Marvin, a really big strong black man, is Manager of Building and Grounds and Maintenance at the La Mancha. His little workshop takes up the back half of the Sand Dollar while the rental offices are in the front. Marvin's age is hard to determine for his life obviously has been hard. He was a Navy

Seal a few years ago and he used to raise hell around Fort Walton Beach as a teenager. He has a younger brother who tends bar and shucks oysters with lightning speed at the Tides Inn and he seems to be the only family Marvin has except for his wife who has never been to the La Mancha as far as I know.

Marvin will absolutely not talk about his life even if asked a direct question. When a group of people is around like when he tends bar at one of our socials, he is jovial and talks about things with a big grin on his face. He's a mystery to me, and of course, he can be anywhere on the property anytime he wants. Many times I have seen him at the big Y shaped pool between Pelican and Dolphin when I go for my early morning walks. Sometimes he will speak, but most of the time he turns abruptly and goes off in another direction.

Something this morning had caused Marvin to act like I had never seen him before. What had caused him to be on the beach, and why was he in such a hurry to get away from me?

It was a beautiful day I thought as I looked down to see Max walking around the corner of the building. It was well past 8:30. He waved up at me and I hollered that I would fix sandwiches for his lunch. He gave me the thumbs-up sign while walking down the ramp of the gazebo.

As Max was putting out the umbrellas spacing them exactly six paces apart, he suddenly threw the four of five he had on his shoulder into the sand twenty feet away and let out a yell. He looked over the bank and then lunged backward and whirled around and coughed up his breakfast in the sand. The seagulls scattered into the air squawking, flapping their wings frantically, and then dropped down once more in a frenzy of pecking.

Max ran for the gazebo shouting for someone to call the police. He made a beeline toward my balcony.

He yelled up at me, "Her body's out there! She's cut all over!"

Then he vomited again. All the macho attitude and piss and vinegar he usually displays drained out of him and he sat down in the grass.

4

A Few Minutes Later

It was almost impossible to explain to Elsie, the dispatcher, that there was a body on the beach at the La Mancha. She kept saying, "That's never happened before! That can't be. We've never had a body on the beach anywhere on Okaloosa Island."

I finally convinced her to get in touch with the deputies.

It seemed like a long time and they hadn't arrived. I figured they were over in Destin at the DoNut Hole and later I found out I was right.

Maybe Elsie had failed to tell them why they needed to get to the La Mancha in a hurry because they stopped a speeding cyclist out on Highway 98 on their way back, and while one of them was out writing the ticket, the other one sat in their SUV with his drawn revolver in his lap. That was their usual 'Motorus Opperendee,' they said.

They had convinced the sheriff somehow that they should ride together and therefore save the county the money of buying two patrol vehicles. He probably agreed to it after one of them had been tied up by a bunch of visiting college girls and he was seen walking down 98 bare assed naked.

Before they did arrive, Gerald our security man came out of his little gate house and stood in the gazebo watching the spot Max had pointed to making sure no one went down there. When the deputies came, Gerald went back into his little house looking very relieved.

The deputies talked to Max there on the lawn as he wouldn't go back down on the beach. I stood listening, and then followed them as they went down to the water. We tried to wave the gulls away, but just made them angry as they started diving at us from all directions. Finally, the deputies got to the edge and looked over. One of them lost his breakfast or maybe it was the donut from the DoNut Hole. The other one just stood cussing in the wind.

I finally got up close and looked over the bank. I wished I hadn't. The gulls had done grisly work on her face as half of it was gone. Her eyes were just gobs of bloody streams. Three or four gulls were still on her pecking new cuts on her at random. Both her arms were missing their hands. One of them had plastic bags fastened on it with bright party like ribbon. The bags had a lot of what looked like congealed blood in them. I felt the coffee coming up and my throat was filled with the sour taste of vomit. She lay there nude with just seaweed wrapped around one leg like a grotesque mermaid.

One of the deputies said, "We can't handle this. This has never happened before...."

The other agreed, "We've got to call it in. God Almighty, did you see her face?

5
Nine o'clock

Brantley had hurried around Dolphin building, rushed into his condo, got dressed in his uniform, and hurried out past the parking lot to the perimeter fence which encircles the La Mancha complex to where he parks his car away from all the others. He removed the canvas cover, folded it and put it into the floor behind the seat, got into his little yellow Porsche, and exited through the pole-gate.

The little Porsche was a yellow streak as he sped along 98. He slowed down when he reached the Pass Bridge and went through the business district of Destin, but went speeding along Airport Road until he saw a patrolman up ahead; then he slowed to 40. When he rushed out to the hanger, he was relieved to find his Beechcraft 77 Skipper was ready for him. He ran over and threw a bag of trash into a dumpster.

He taxied down the runway and the plane took off with a roar. He loved this old plane. It was getting harder and harder to get parts for it as only 312 of them had ever been made, and he knew he would have to part with her before long.

He was late. He was scheduled to be in Mobile at noon. He had to get his pride-and-joy yellow Sikorsky copter ready when he got there. If he remembered correctly he had left it without much fuel the last time he came in and since he was the only pilot, it would have to be fueled. He would make a general inspection and question Seth the mechanic if he suspected anything needed repair.

He was pleased that his Porsche, Beechcraft, and the Sikorsky were all yellow. Brantley liked consistency.

He was to take off for a rig in the Gulf with three company officials at 1:30. He guessed it would be an absolute miracle if he was ready.

He knew he should be flying out over the Gulf since it was only a hundred miles or so if he did, but he wanted to go down 98 to see if Ryan was at home. He throttled back and almost followed Highway 98 back over Okaloosa Island and then over Fort Walton Beach. Far out to his left he saw a commotion on the beach at the La Mancha, and his hands gripped the wheel tighter. "Oh, shit," he said out loud as he saw the police cars parked down on the lawn by the pool. He shook uncontrollably for a second thinking how much trouble he would be in if anyone decided to go into his condo.

As he went past Fort Walton, he saw the produce stand alongside the road and the little airstrip right beside it. The lane that ran down the side of the strip ended at the Sound where Ryan Tilley his friend, maybe his only friend, lived. A Waco YMF5 open cockpit bi-plane—an old crop duster--was taking off and Brantley dipped his wing as he saw Ryan in the Waco. His spirits lifted as Ryan waved at him as he flew by.

Brantley thought Ryan was an ace when it came to women. He had a laid-back country charm that women found interesting, and Brantley knew he had trouble communicating with women so he hung around with Ryan. Their relationship was somewhat one-sided as he realized he was always the one to call and suggest they do something together. He remembered when he had suggested, and then pestered Ryan, that they go to Launie's. Ryan was embarrassed when they talked about it afterward.

He was nearly over Pensacola when two Navy copters appeared from out of nowhere coming at him. He almost pissed his pants for he knew he was in their flight pattern. He turned the Beechcraft sharply to the left as he should have, and the copters went whizzing by.

One of the pilots gave him the finger as they quickly disappeared.

6
Eleven o'clock

Detective Emile Morat arrived at eleven. Morat moved to the area from up north about ten years ago; by up north, I mean somewhere in Georgia. He had been in police work all his life, but he had never succeeded and missed out when promotion times came around. When he moved to Okaloosa County, the detective who had done work for the county for years had retired. Morat applied for the job and got it.

I'm not saying the title of 'Detective' went to his head, but he always frowns when someone doesn't address him as Detective Morat. He dresses, no matter how hot or cold it is, in long white polyester pants. I don't know how many pairs of them he has but either he bought a dozen pairs when they went out of style, or his wife Libby washes them every night. He claims to be French and thinks he might look like Paul Henreid. He's a slight little man not over five feet six or seven and probably was good looking twenty years ago. I would bet he's seen Casablanca a hundred times. He will often lower his voice, and with his best Henreid accent quote lines from it.

He has a habit of eating those little foil wrapped chocolate kisses like he works for the company that makes them. He always has a pocket full of them, and leaves a trail of foil wherever he goes.

I'm not certain how it happened, but I had seen to it that the area was roped off and no one came near the place where the body was. Ironically, the same rope was used last night to rope off an area of the beach for a wedding.

The coroner and his photographer arrived with Morat. The photographer took hundreds of pictures getting wet from the waist down as she got out into the water to get that angle. Morat, the coroner, and I had to continually wave our arms frantically to keep the gulls at bay. Doc Wells, the coroner, formally pronounced the woman dead but he and Morat went over the area again and again. Dr. Wells, a wise older doctor who had stopped his own medical practice when he became coroner, kept telling Morat there was nothing else to be seen on the beach, but Morat walked the area again and again and once I thought he was going to take off his shoes and get into the water.

I heard several of the tourists on the beach talking about how it was indecent to leave her body half in and half out of the water as long as Morat was taking. One woman went up to him and shouted he should be ashamed of himself, "She's someone's daughter, you know."

I also heard some of them saying they were checking out. I heard one father say, "We can't stay here after the kids have seen all this."

Over an hour later the two medics encased the now bright red sunburned body in a body bag along with lots of seaweed and sand. They loaded it on a gurney and struggled with the load up across the sand, climbed the ramp up to the gazebo and went down the boardwalk where they loaded it into the ambulance parked there on the lawn. The coroner and his crew drove away with the body.

Morat was not likely to find much of anything where the body had been found because Kelsey, the De Paul University girl who drives the big green John Deere tractor with the clanking sand rake attached to the back, had made her laps as she does each morning from way down at Anglers Pier in the east to the fence at the west end of La Mancha's property. She stops the tractor along the way, empties the big trash cans into the back of the rake, and continues on to do the same all the way down the beach.

The sun set with just as magnificent a sunset as usual disregarding the horrific happenings today at the La Mancha. Another storm must have occurred somewhere out past the horizon for the waves, four to five feet tall now, were slapping the sand with loud pops.

Jonathan L sat on his post with his head drooped on his breast.

7

Twelve Years Earlier

Paul Bishop and his mother Trish live over in Seagull on the sixth floor. Trish bought the condo because events changed Paul's life on September 11, 2001. Paul was four years old then and they lived in Destin where he was a preschooler at Destin Elementary. He was a proud 'Dolphin.'

Paul and his dad virtually lived on the beach when his dad was home. They swam together and his dad called him 'Frog' for a long time because Paul would jump into the warm Gulf water, go under, and swim for yards pumping his little legs like a frog before finally surfacing. He was ecstatic when his dad let him take the controls of their little fishing boat. A picture still hangs in his bedroom of the Red Snapper he caught just outside the Pass at Destin. His dad is in the background of the picture and has a grin that makes Paul proud, but sad.

Matt, his dad, was a pilot for American Airlines and during the summer of Paul's fourth year the family had flown to Hawaii for two weeks of pure happiness for Paul. He marveled at how the beaches and water around the islands of Hawaii were so different than the sands and water of the Gulf. He was already so conscious of the waters of the seas.

They had moved to Destin so the family could be at the beach and also to be away from 'big city life' as Matt had said. Matt would board an Air Tram flight out of Valparaiso where the North West Regional Airport is, fly to Atlanta and be off to whatever his next flight assignment was leaving on the same day most of the time.

He and Paul had talked a long time on the night of September 10. The last thing Matt had said was, 'Be the man!' He had said it in a light-hearted playful way but the words would haunt Paul the rest of his life.

Trish dropped Paul in front of the Dolphin sculpture at Destin Elementary the next morning. She kissed the top of his head as he turned in the seat to unfasten his seat belt. They both knew he shouldn't be riding in the front seat, and he knew no one better not see her kissing him goodbye. That was his rule.

At nine o'clock, Grammy Helen, his mom's mother, came to the office and he was called out of class. All the kids had heard about the happenings in New York and Washington because the teachers were upset and talking among themselves. Paul was afraid something was bad wrong.

Because of the tragic happenings of September 11 and how the Nation was affected, little coverage or attention was given to the Air Tram flight which crashed near Big Swamp Creek north of Valparaiso that morning. All on board the little twenty passenger plane had died in the crash or drowned in the swamp.

Paul missed school until the first week of October. The funeral was a horrible sad blur for him that he didn't understand. The only thing he did understand was that his dad was gone. Trish tried all she could to do some of the things he and his dad had done together, but it didn't work. Paul had horrible dreams and had no interest in doing anything.

He changed at Christmas when he brought Trish a card that he made the night before in his room. She opened it and burst into tears. He wrapped his little arms around her bent over head. His card simply said, "I'm the man." He would take care of her nearly to the end of his life.

From the Christmas holiday, Paul's attitude and determination changed. He became the best student in school where grades were concerned. His teachers were amazed he knew much more than a four year old should. He shadowed his mother wherever she went, always there to open her door or to carry groceries which were much too heavy for him.

Elementary and Middle School were a breeze for Paul. He excelled at everything from Science to running track. He was on the State Middle School Cross Country winning team with his close friend, Sam, and the other runners. 'Little' Destin Middle School had been laughed at when they qualified for the State Meet. Only one school at the event down in Lakeland had fewer students than Destin. Coach Mac had told them they would probably be called nobodies from the Panhandle, but when the competition was over, they had shown the state where Destin is. Paul was so proud of his team, but never said anything about his first place finish. That was just his nature.

He graduated from Destin Middle School, and he and Trish had to decide where he would go to high school as there is no high school at Destin. They choose Fort Walton Beach High.

At the beginning of Paul's freshman year, Trish and he looked at condos on Okaloosa Island. They finally chose the one in the Seagull at the La Mancha after seeing many newer ones up and down the Blvd because they liked the solitude of the place.

8

Brantley

Brantley had one three week period of his young life when he was completely happy. He was eleven that year when his Uncle Jim came to Florida from his big farm in Oregon. He had asked Brantley's mom if Brantley might go with him on his trip to Zimbabwe. Brantley was amazed when he found out about it and that she had agreed he could go.

He spent the rest of the week in excited anticipation. Uncle Jim was younger than his mom, a bachelor who had left Pensacola when he was nineteen to see the West. He had ended up in Oregon, had eventually bought a huge plot of land and was growing those luscious yellow and peach colored cherries. Brantley had no idea how he had made his money to buy the place, and, of course, he had only seen pictures of it. Jim brought a large wooden crate of the cherries with him; Brantley ate so many he almost got sick. Uncle Jim was going to Zimbabwe to visit his college roommate—they had been Ducks at the University of Oregon.

The morning they were to take Jim's rental car over to Valparaiso to fly the American Eagle to Atlanta where they would board the big 787 for Harare, Brantley's mom had given him some money. He was very surprised for she never gave him money; she bought what she thought he deserved. She said, "Buy one of those Desert Pith Helmets." He was startled but knew he would have to obey and buy it.

They stayed in a remarkable home where there was no glass in the windows but netting was stretched over the window frames. Brantley had a room to himself on the second floor and one morning he awoke to find a giraffe had torn away the netting and was standing with its head sticking into his room. He thought that was the coolest thing that had ever happened to him until they took a big Land Rover and traveled several miles across the plains. He saw animals he had never seen except in pictures. A monkey had approached at lunch time and had jumped on Brantley's shoulder to grab bread Brantley was eating. Brantley hadn't flinched when the monkey landed on his shoulder, and for the rest of the trip he was called 'Bwana!' Brantley was in heaven. No one ever told him the monkey was a pet belonging to one of the guides.

At the airport in Harare on their way home, Brantley found the Pith Helmet he would wear for much of his life. He knew he better not go home without a present for his mom, so Uncle Jim gave him money and he bought a beautiful cut bottle that was filled with Jasmine perfume.

When they had deplaned in Atlanta, Uncle Jim took him to the gate for the flight to Valparaiso, hugged him tight and shook his hand. Brantley felt so grown up as he told his uncle how much the last three weeks had meant to him. He had tears in his eyes as the little American Eagle took off and he was headed home.

As the plane flew over Fort Walton Beach to land at Valparaiso, Brantley shook with dread. A grandmother type sitting across the narrow aisle from him reached over and patted his arm and assured him they would land safely. That wasn't why Brantley was shaking.

The lady at the ticket counter met him and walked him out to the taxi which would take him home to his mother.

She seemed sincerely glad to see him and gave him a hug when he presented her the bottle of perfume. She loved it, she said. Brantley would smell that smell for the rest of his life.

She laughed when he tried on the Pith Helmet and he announced he was to be called 'Bwana.'

He carried his bag into his bedroom and was a little surprised to find a new piece of furniture standing against one wall. His mom had bought a wardrobe which was huge reaching clear to the ceiling and was sturdy and thick. He would find out it was also almost sound proof.

Brantley wet the bed that night and the next day spent his first time in the wardrobe. He vomited three times during the day. In the tight space he couldn't raise his arms and his vomit ran down his chest.

When she let him out, the sun was going down. He crumpled to the floor. She leaned over and helped him to his feet and pushed him into the bathroom, stripped him naked and soaped his entire body as he stood shivering. After she had thoroughly dried his body, he returned to his room and found the first of many pairs of little black Speedos.

9

Paul

Living at the La Mancha was like being next to the gates of Paradise for Paul because he was only yards from the beach and his friends spent the weekends with him to ride their boards in the water, disturb Jonathan away from the volleyball net as they competed in a wild and competitive game, or just lie in the sand. He seemed to belong to the water as he was skillful in any activity he tried.

As he had grown, he became a striking young man and the girls at Fort Walton High were suddenly spending much time on our beachfront. I had met Trish and Paul when they first moved here so often when school was in session he would come to my condo so I could help him with his essays or to discuss whatever novel he was reading in English at FWBH.

I gave him *Jonathan Livingstone Seagull* by Richard Bach on one of his birthdays; he had laughed as he said, "Gee, Finally a thin book! Thanks!" One afternoon after he had finished it, he knocked on my door and as I let him in, he suddenly hugged me real tight. He had tears in his eyes as he said, "Thanks for the wonderful book!" He spun around and I didn't see him for a couple of days.

I had already named Jonathan L seagull which sits on the volleyball goal post. After Paul's trip to my condo about the book I would see him many times sitting on the low white stone wall which surrounds La Mancha's property where he was very close to Jonathan L.

The day before Max discovered the body Paul was sitting looking out over the Gulf in that favorite spot when he spied what seemed to be a live plastic grocery sack. He walked down the boardwalk past the gazebo and over the sand to where the sack was thrashing about. There seemed to be a battle going on inside it.

He kicked it with his bare foot and several blue crabs scampered out and raced backwards down the sand snapping their big front claws all the way into the water.

As they were getting out of the bag it had ripped open so Paul could see the remains of what looked like some kind of fish. As he leaned down and read the bag he saw it was from a store he had never heard of, Piggly Wiggly, and he wondered from what other state this might have come all the way to his beach. He scooped up the bag and its messy contents on a piece of drift wood he had seen washed onto the beach earlier and threw them into the big beach trash barrel.

As he turned to go back up to the lawn, he saw a beautiful big blue and white yacht glide by way out on the water. He stood amazed at its beauty and realizing its power as he imagined the adventures he could have on a boat like that.

10
Ryan

One of the diversions of the day is the little plane flying over the beach at a low altitude with banners attached to its tail which advertise 'TIDES INN BEST SEA FOOD THERE IS' or 'HELLEN BACK PIZZA' or 'CALVINS'S ISLAND EVERYTHING 75% OFF.' All three of these businesses are located on Okaloosa Island and I wonder how much business that plane brings in?

Ryan Tilley was pulling the 'TIDES INN...' banner this morning and as he waved to Brantley he wondered why Brantley was flying down the highway, the Miracle Strip as we call it, but he turned up his Bose Sport headphones his mother had sent him last Christmas above the drone of his little open cockpit plane and kept an eye out for planes coming out of Eglin.

He had not worked the last two days but had gone to Panama City to see his mom. He didn't remember having as much fuel in his plane as the gage showed. He would certainly remember that, he thought, as expensive as fuel is. Also, what was that unusual smell in the air?

He planned to circle down to Destin and fly by several times, then back up to Fort Walton and do the same, and especially over Okaloosa Island to make sure the people at Tides Inn saw him. Then he would return to the little airstrip where his buddy Freddie, the nineteen year old who ran his produce stand up the lane on Highway 98, would have the next banner ready for him to bolt to the rigging at the back of the plane. He would drop the Tides Inn banner, attach the new one on the tail and fly the patterns all over again.

Ryan and Brantley had grown up together, gone to Fort Walton Beach High, and got together at Tides Inn about once a week. The Inn has fresh catch of the day, maybe the best raw oysters in the area, and a bunch of cute young waitresses. One in particular caught both their eyes. She was new, from over in Mississippi they heard and really paid attention to them when they went in to eat and drink. She was attractive in a subtle way, not drop dead gorgeous, but really pretty.

She was a striking blonde with green eyes that reminded Ryan of the Gulf water and a clear complexion that Brantley called 'Georgia peach!' Ryan was aching to ask her out and Brantley claimed he was too, but neither wanted to be turned down for the other one to find out about, so they just kept admiring her and building up the nerve to ask her.

Ryan was thinking of her as he cruised over Tides Inn circling several times. He made another circle going out further this time and saw quite a commotion on the beach at the La Mancha. There were several police vehicles in the parking lot and an emergency vehicle on the lawn just next to the gazebo at the end of the boardwalk. He circled again just to see what he could.

11

The Day after the Body

Max isn't at work this morning. Morat had said he was pretty shook up yesterday, but it just might be he has the day off. I had told Morat that Max was not at work when he said he was. I hope it doesn't cause him problems, and I had also told Morat that Max had probably stopped at the Tom Thumb halfway down Santa Rosa Blvd under the guise of getting a Gator Ade, but really to see and talk with one of the cashiers he was after. He is twenty-three after all.

Morat sat in the gazebo most of the day. I was in and out of my condo but I never saw him move. He sat on the bench facing the Gulf as if deeming the answer to the body to come to him. I half-way expected the *La Marseillaise* to come blaring out and down the boardwalk. If we had thought Brantley was strange, we hadn't met Morat yet. It was late June and it was hot, but he wore those white poly pants and had recently tied a bright red scarf around his neck.

Tourists would stop and give him a double take and I imagine wonder if they had chosen the right condo complex for their vacations. One old lady sat down by him and tried to speak to him in French, but he didn't understand her.

He and Trooper J C Blevins sat in silence it seemed to me, but Bicycle Bob told me later Morat had asked him about Piggly Wiggly stores in the area.

Bob is a native of the Panhandle, grew up in Pensacola, and the family had moved to Fort Walton Beach when he entered high school. He graduated from Choctaw High School, the intercity arch rival of FWBH.

"Little" Bob Bakersfield had made a name for himself as a running back in the state of Florida.

Now, he certainly couldn't be called 'little' as the bicycle he is always riding seems to disappear under his large bulk, and either he shaves his head or is naturally bald. I think he is naturally bald.

His heart is as big as his body and his laugh is infectious, so Bob is one of the best liked residents of the La Mancha. His bicycle has a 'Groucho Marks' horn on it that he squeezes with abandonment when he sees a friend. There isn't a party until Bob arrives!

He said he told Morat that years ago there was a Piggly Wiggly out on Elgin Parkway in Fort Walton but it had been closed long ago. He said that Blevins had called in to check if there were any PW's left in the Panhandle and got word back while they were still talking that the closest one was way down past Panama City at St. Joe which is over seventy miles away.

When I walked down the boardwalk to the ramp at the gazebo this morning, Morat was sitting in the dark in the gazebo. He startled me being there so early in the morning.

"You seen Brantley?"

"No, I haven't seen him since that morning... But, sometimes he is gone for days. I remember once when he was gone a month."

"Call me if you see him."

He walked over to lean on the railing and gazed out at the Gulf as I went down the ramp to walk west toward the warning sign of the Air Command. I hadn't walked at my usual before dawn time this morning because of all the chaos going on around the complex, but I went now just to get away.

12

Tutoring Paul

I had never tutored a student one-on-one before, so Paul became very important to me. I either went to their condo where Trish always fed me a delicious meal, or Paul came to my condo where we would talk for hours about a novel or an essay assignment and then go out on my balcony and talk about life.

That night after we had talked about the body and the confusion and fear around La Mancha, we talked about Twain's Huck. The passage which was on Paul's mind was when Huck has the dilemma about whether to turn in Jim, the black slave who is escaping down the Mississippi River with Huck on the raft. It is actually the climax, or Huck's decision is, of the coming-of-age novel.

Paul will be a senior this fall and he was already the backup quarterback for FWBH's football team. He and his best buddy, Chris Duggins, are two fine quarterbacks who will vie for the starting position. The Bishop and Doogs are inseparable. You see one of them and the other one will walk around the corner in a few seconds.

He is taking Mrs. Fleming's AP Seminar on Twain this summer so he will have one less class in the fall. We had talked about Huckleberry Finn for many nights for it is a long complicated novel and Mrs. Fleming is milking it dry as she usually does. Paul understood it was Huck's adventure of becoming a man, in making his own decisions, and he saw himself in many of the same situations.

And then he wanted to talk about the dilemma of Huck turning Jim in or not. He had said the quote several times, "'Ok, I'll just go to Hell,' Huck had hollered when he had decided to not turn in Jim…." Paul understood the book and what the quote meant, but he was not interested in that. He was trying to decide if he would do the same for a friend.

I asked, "You mean Doogs?"

"Yeah....."

"Why, is Doogs doing something you think he should not be doing?"

"No, no, I don't mean that. I just wonder if I would stand up for him like Huck did for Jim. Or, would I stand up for someone who was being treated wrong."

"I think you would."

And I let the matter go. I had encountered many students in my teaching career and listened to many 'secrets,' and I knew Paul wasn't ready to talk about whatever he thought was right or wrong.

He told me good night and said, "Don't walk the beach early in the morning like you always do. I don't think it's safe."

13

I Remember

I didn't go down to the beach this morning, but took my Folgers out on the balcony about the same time as usual. All seems ordinary except for the big section still blocked off with yellow police tape per Morat's instructions.

I watch through my binoculars three great blue herons glide onto the beach making perfect two-point running landings. Remarkably, they are all spaced about like Max had schooled them in how well symmetry makes the beach look with his umbrellas and beach chairs. They strut on west pecking in the sand occasionally with their long sharp beaks. Magnificent birds!

The morning sky is filled with orange tinted clouds as the sun is up over the water at Destin. Our Air Patrol of Brown Pelicans makes its fly-over in correct V formation. A school of dolphins is trolling up and down about a hundred yards out.

The herons take off—one, two, and three—spaced like planes waiting their turn on the tarmac. They swoop out across the water and glide into shore a little farther west. I turn my attention back to the dolphins that are seriously fishing up and down a stretch of water.

Three kayakers are trying to intercept the dolphins as the little pod heads west. Just as they arrive to where they think the dolphins should be, I laugh out loud as I see fins surface at least a hundred yards farther on. Through my binoculars I see one of the kayakers throw up his hands in defeat, but over his head I see that beautiful blue and white boat—then I see it wasn't just a boat, but a very powerful expensive yacht-- about two or three hundred yards beyond him.

I remember what I hadn't told Morat. I had seen that large blue and white boat one morning a few days ago going back and forth about a quarter of a mile out. I'm bad at judging distance on the water, so I may be way off on how far out it was, but it had traveled from east to west and had gone back and forth twice. It was traveling very slowly like it was trolling for fish or looking for something and it was doing the same right now.

Morat arrived as I came back out with my cell phone aiming to call him, and he had Trooper Blevins with him. Morat saw me and hollered and asked me to come down to the gazebo.

"Look out on the water at that big boat," I shouted waving my arm and pointing out toward the water.

But as I pointed, the boat was nowhere to be seen. It had disappeared as I went to get my cell phone, I guess.

I had told him everything I knew yesterday except for the boat I now remembered. As I went down on the elevator, I wondered what he might want.

"You didn't level with me yesterday. Why?"

I told him about the boat out in the Gulf which had slipped my mind and that it was there just now.

"You see it clear enough to see a name?"

"No, I couldn't see that. It was pretty far out."

"We'll check it out. But that's not what you didn't tell me. Who's Walkin Al?"

I smiled, but he didn't, and I quickly said I didn't say anything about Al because he's out just like me walking around the property and sometimes on the beach. Only I said Al usually walks in the late afternoon so that he sees the sunset from the gazebo. I told Morat I seldom see Al on the beach itself.

"Who is that? Bicycle Bob and now Walkin Al... You all have some weird names for people."

"I don't know his last name, but everyone who lives here calls him Walkin Al. He's older than I am, but has a bevy of girlfriends who call or text him hourly. I hear he likes women much younger than him. They would have to be because he's older than I am, but he is really robust and strong. I can't keep up with him when I try to walk with him. He travels a lot, just got back from India, and is planning a trip to the Greek Islands."

"How do you know so damn much?"

"Because we sit around the pool and talk about things. He was there the other afternoon and told us all about his trips. One of the women was teasing him about his 'women friends.' He got a call at that very moment, looked a little embarrassed but said he could talk. We had heard him say he would see her later that night as he walked away and we had all laughed."

"What time were you down on the beach this morning?"

"I didn't go walking this morning."

"Why? You do this walking every day?"

"Unless it's storming, and I have been known to walk in the rain. But I didn't this morning."

"Why?"

"Well, Morat, with all that has happened, I just didn't feel like it."

He glared at me, but said, "And that morning, you saw nothing strange?"

"Well, there was Brantley..."

"Trying to be funny? I heard you thought I am gullible."

"No sir, but you must admit Brantley is unusual..."

"I don't know because I haven't met him. He seems to have disappeared."

"I'm certain I told you that he was gone for days at a time..."

"Yeah, but why now?"

14

The Lollipop

The *NorthWest Daily* ran the story with a banner headline on the front page the next morning:

Body of nude woman found at water's edge at the La Mancha on the Island.

Believed to be in her twenties, she was tangled in seaweed and her face had been mutilated by seagulls, Detective Emile Morat reported. She, of course, had no identification on her, and because of the mutilation of her face, it is hard to determine her features. In addition, both her arms had been cut off in jagged hacks between her elbows and her wrists. She appears to have been blonde, but her hair may have been dyed. If anyone has information about a missing woman in her twenties or thirties, it is important you contact the Okaloosa County Sheriff and ask for Detective Morat. The department really needs help with this.

I was on my balcony, drinking my coffee out of Winnie the Pooh which I had chipped this morning, and reading the Daily. I was thinking it was not much of a story, but how could it be? Morat was really frustrated and even though I do think he is really gullible, he didn't have a clue as to how this murder happened.

The Air Patrol flew over. How do those so graceful-in-the-sky birds become the awkward wobbling swaying clowns weaving across a pier—sometimes even falling over? They were in perfect V formation as usual, and I wonder how they select the leader and just how the others know when to fall into formation.

Just as I was seeing the last of the pelicans disappear over the top of my building, something caught my eye and I saw it again. There is was much closer into shore than the other day and I am sure it's the same boat. I grabbed my binoculars and focused in on it. It wasn't a fishing boat as I had once thought but a large white yacht with blue trim. I made out the name, *Lollipop*, I thought as I watched it speed away back to the west toward Pensacola. I lost sight of it as the end of the Dolphin building blocked my view.

I called Morat and told him what I had seen. I was so thankful he answered the phone, and I didn't have to go through Elsie. Trooper Blevins was with him and Morat gave him the information.

I heard the trooper say, "I know that boat. We all do. It docks over in Pensacola. Belongs to Launie Sanderson… That thing is probably worth a half-million or so. Launie takes care of it like she does one of her girls. Strange…it would be cruising around over here."

Before Morat hung up, he asked if I had seen Brantley. I told him no, and then he said he would see me this afternoon. I'm getting a little tired of all his questions.

The *Daily* article caused quite a stir around the complex. Max was very busy renting out chairs and umbrellas to almost anyone. Then they would ask him the question, "What did you see?" and he would pocket their money and say, "Detective Morat has ordered me to be quiet." The chairs and umbrellas suddenly were emptied, and those who were brave enough edged up to look over the police tape as close as they dared.

Max made some good easy money! But, Daniel, his boss finally came and told him to take the rest of the day off because everyone was bothering him so. I'm glad my name never came up in the conversations.

When Morat came, the first question was the same one I had answered too many times already. "Did you see anyone that morning?"

"I told you several times that I didn't…not down to the east or here at the La Mancha."

"Well, let's hear you tell it again. You did say there were lights on in the Pelican and the Dolphin buildings that morning."

"Yes, and there were people sitting out on their balconies waiting for the sun to rise, or drinking coffee, or just sitting, I guess."

"Which balconies?"

What an absolute ditz, I thought. How about you look up at the buildings and tell me the unit numbers. All you see are the balconies. Get those chocolate kisses out of your pie hole, and use your head. But I said, "I have no idea."

The La Mancha is a complex of six large buildings which at one time really looked Spanish. They had clay Spanish tiled roofs and still are painted stark white.

Bicycle Bob had told me that Ivan destroyed most of the roofs, filled the big pool that is between the Pelican and the Dolphin with sand and broken roof, rock and balcony railings. He said it took a crew of a dozen or so men with a backhoe and two dump trucks nearly a week to get the tons of sand out of the big pool.

The pool fence which is several feet higher than the perimeter fence had nearly all been swept into the pool with the sand and had made the job that much more difficult.

The roofs have been reroofed with metal which looks very much like Spanish tile, but those who have lived here a long time say, "It's just not the same." The buildings are all white; whiter than even the sand on our beach. The balconies have ornate railings made of precast sections which have been installed to look like medieval Spain.

The Pelican and the Dolphin, like all the other buildings, are six stories tall and each floor has ten condos. The two buildings form a V shape with a lawn between them which may be eighty to a hundred yards wide at the narrow end of the V. The pool is between them positioned up against the low stone perimeter wall near the dunes which divide the complex from the beach. A boardwalk runs down to the gazebo on the east end and another boardwalk goes to the beach on the west end butting up against the high dilapidated chained-linked fence. Jagged holes appear in many places along the old fence and at one point it is ripped apart from the top almost down to the ground. Barbed wire is stretched along the top; it designates the beginning of the Air Command's property.

The body was found a few yards west of the gazebo at the water's edge.

Morat uttered something I didn't hear, and said to the two deputies and Trooper Blevins, "Damn, we'll have to question all of them."

The two deputies looked like they had been hit with something. I wondered just how well they would ask questions. But that wasn't Morat's plan. He stationed himself and Blevins at one of the tables at the pool. He had a bowl of those little kisses on the table, and I thought he was going to slap Blevins' hand when he reached for one.

He and Blevins and the person being questioned would be sitting in the shade of the umbrella while the deputies went from floor to floor of each building trying to rouse the residents. It would take a long time for on top of everything else, our elevators are slow.

Of course, the plan was completely silly from the beginning. I kept my silence but was laughing at the gullibility of Morat. Many of the people who were here yesterday are gone now. There had been a large group of young people from Ohio, I believe, who were on some kind of retreat. There was a large wedding party from Oklahoma and Missouri and they are gone.

There are all those people who had gone because of the horrific mess on the beach, and, of course, new people had moved in this morning. Many of the regular residents who live here all the time were gone to work. Besides that, I nearly laughed at the idea of someone admitting they saw or had some part of what happened.

My entertainment for the day was the gulls. They apparently smelled the chocolate kisses in the bowl on Morat's table. They appeared to be working in groups as two or three would swoop in together and while some hovered over his head, some others managed to turn the bowl over and escape with the foil wrapped goodies. Morat finally emptied what was left into one of his shirt pockets. But the gulls continued to swoop in at him and J C squawking loudly.

Someone did tell Morat that Brantley had flown some company people out to a rig and would be gone for over a week. When Blevins called the woman in the company office in Mobile she wasn't sure how many rigs they would be on or just exactly where they would be each day. She said they would call in each day as to where they could be that day.

Morat was incensed. His little French face turned crimson and he sputtered.

15

Brantley, the Hero

Brantley spent over a month in late April and early May in 2010 flying to many rigs in the Gulf with concerned company officials.

On April 10, one of British Petroleum's rigs exploded causing a disaster for the Gulf Coast like mankind had never seen before. All the 2600 or so oil rigs belonging to many companies have been given names, and the Deepwater Horizon exploded killing eleven men who worked it. It sank into the Gulf two days later, but for months millions of gallons of oil spewed up into the water. Currents carried the long stringy ropes of oil straight to the many beaches of Louisiana, Mississippi, Alabama, and Florida.

Soon the whole world was seeing underwater pictures of the oil still gushing up into the Gulf and as the cameras went to the surface we saw live pictures of devastated marshlands, dead and dying sea life, hundreds of thousands of birds and small animals dying in sticky coats of the thick black oil. The lowlands and the beaches which were the pride and economic life of so many beachside towns soon were outlined with globs of the gooey mess.

Compared to the three other states involved, we were lucky. We did have globs of the thick oil wash up on our beaches and we spent many hours scooping up the stuff and patrolling for it. Our main disaster was we lost much of our income because the tourists didn't come on their vacations with us.

Brantley's company decided that to show the world its concern, it would fly company inspectors out in the bright yellow Sikorsky with an accompanying news helicopter to send back publicity pictures for the folks at home to see their concern.

As he landed his Beechcraft at the Destin Airport after one of those trips, Brantley was relieved to see his little Porsche still sitting under the canopy he had had built there and still covered with the heavy canvas cover. He had secured his plane, walked to the Porsche, and was soon sitting in the soft leather seat. He breathed deeply and then a jolt of dread filled his stomach and he was almost sick. He had spent six weeks flying from rig to Mobile and then back to some other rig in the Gulf, and his demeanor and confident gave him a sense of wellbeing and worth, but now that he was nearly home, he was filled with dread and anxiety, but the dread was clearly the strongest.

He stopped at a flower shop and bought a dozen yellow roses thinking flowers would earn him some points with his mom and that his first day home would be bearable.

He was wrong. As he entered their condo, he smelled fresh baked cookies. Why had he ever let her know he was coming? He knew they were oatmeal raisin cookies, his favorite. He also knew what they would cause for him. His mother was dressed in that old-fashioned 1950's house dress. She smiled and as she approached to kiss his cheek, he shuddered.

"Welcome home, Brantley!"

She was a small slender woman who looked frail at first glance, but even in her fifties she was stout and the muscles in her arms corded when she lifted something heavy.

"I've made your favorite cookies, Brantley. See they're on the table with the glass of milk. Now, sit and I will tuck the napkin into your shirt so you won't get your uniform stained."

Although he was twenty-six years old, Brantley was terrified of his mother. She knew, as only she could, his secret. She controlled him because of it.

He sat, and like a little boy told to stay at the table until his plate was clean, it was several minutes later he had choked down the cookies and milk.

"Now it's time for your bath, sweetie."

She pulled him into his room and closed the door. When he whirled around, she stood between him and the door. From a chest top she picked up his Pith Helmet and put it on her own head; in the crook of one arm, she held the dozen yellow roses. She grabbed his arms and started a weird and eerie humming as she caused them to circle around and around.

On the second time around Brantley saw the open door of the wardrobe. She didn't see the unusual hard expression that came over his face as she was holding him almost against herself now. As they revolved the third time when she was directly in front of the open wardrobe, he shoved her inside and slammed the door. He turned the key in the lock.

The last thing he heard was her interrupted surprised scream of rage, "Brant..."

The next morning he dared to open the wardrobe. He remembered that when she locked him in and then opened the door that he would fall out into whatever was in front of it because his legs would be asleep. Carefully he opened the door and she slumped against it.

Brantley screamed like a baby as he realized she was dead. He hadn't meant for her to die. She had left him in there overnight several times. He struggled with all his strength to keep her from falling out on top of him. He stood that way for what seemed five minutes and a plan slowly evolved in his head.

How would he ever explain this to anyone? How would he explain the reason? He had to keep it secret from everyone—he would say she had gone away.

Leaning with all his weight, he managed to get his belt off. After faltering several times and almost giving up, he got the belt around her neck. He looped it up over the rod that ran along the top and with all his strength he pulled her back up.

He almost decided to get the pith helmet but he had another idea as his rage returned as he remembered all the times she had tormented and punished him. He got the paint she always used to paint it in completely silly designs in order to humiliate him. Brantley painted a very special message on it.

He knew he would have to find another helmet as everyone around La Mancha would expect him to be wearing one. He thought about the Army Surplus store over on Beale Parkway and then Ebay flashed through his mind.

He closed the door, locked it, hung the key on the nail she had driven into the door, and collapsed on the floor.

A few minutes later, he went in the kitchen, got the can of Pledge and a cloth to polish the wardrobe for the first time.

Later he called several seafood places and finally found one that had a big whole Grouper. He picked it up, took it home, and after taking several shelves out to make room for it, pushed it into the refrigerator.

He took a shower and put on a clean uniform.

As he left the condo, he made sure the refrigerator door was open a few inches. He locked the condo, headed to the airport, got his Beechcraft and left for Mobile for a month.

16

Launie's Domain

Like many tourist areas around the country, Fort Walton Beach has its seedy part of town. Ours is out on the Sound side of Highway 98 where Santa Rosa Blvd crosses 98. Launie Sanderson owns the place. Launie is from New Orleans, and when Katrina demolished her 'establishment' there, she moved her girls, Chuck, and Ollie to Fort Walton Beach. The city fought her a long time trying every legal procedure possible to keep her likes and her kind of business out of town, but she had found a seller and a local person who has a lot of influence in Fort Walton Beach to help her, bought about three acres, and opened up Launie's Gentlemen's Library.

She and her girls live in an old beach house which was already on the property. We call it The Dorm. Once she was here and behaved herself for a couple of years, she and her bunch are tolerated. I imagine she pays a lot of money to someone because she is never raided or inspected that any of us know about.

Launie is a loud-mouthed painted frowning woman most of the time. It would be hard to put an age on her, as her hair changes colors at her whims, and her face reminds me of a painted Japanese geisha. She must be in her fifties but she has started to sag in the wrong places. Her face looks like she was burned badly sometime which may be why she conceals it with so much make-up. Her massive breasts are supported with a bra I've seen on television as able to support the biggest. I know that because of the tops she wears—those that have thin straps. I've never seen her in a top which doesn't emphasize their size.

The sign outside the Library has a picture of her taken years ago. Even then she was 'full-figured' as the ads say, but she was not heavy. Now, she wears loose fitting skirts or pants and her thighs look like they are fighting in a sack. I don't imagine she exercises much and probably sits around a lot, for her back side is wide as 'two axe handles' as my grandpa used to say. She actually looks like that Disney villain from that movie about the little mermaid. Launie chain smokes Winston Lites so her nails are stained with nicotine. A manicurist visits her once a week to apply new fake nails which are nearly always painted with miniature beach scenes. She's nearly six feet tall and I'm guessing at one time back before she let herself go, she was the main attraction at a strip joint like the one she now owns.

Chuck Jenkins, who she calls her foreman, also drives her around in her Cadillac but not in the old fashioned chauffer way because she sits in the front seat. He also pilots her yacht, the *Lollipop*. I've seen Chuck at Tides Inn several times where I usually eat lunch. One day I was finishing my meal when Chuck came in. His order arrived at his table when some of the girls, who are now recognized by most of us as 'Launie's girls' came in. Chuck put down his fork, left money by his plate and walked out. I have never seen him with any of them and I have a feeling there is bad blood between him and all of them.

He doesn't look like he belongs in Launie's entourage. He's a clean-cut young man, probably in his late twenties or early thirties, very handsome, and wears very expensive clothes. Like almost every other man on the Gulf I've never seen him in a suit, but he wears expensive sportswear. According to what's been said after he leaves the Tides Inn at lunch, he all decked out in Polo, Diesel, and True Religion. It makes no difference to me, and I don't know anything about those clothes, except Polo, but all the wait staff sure do notice.

While I was having an oyster Po Boy at Tides Inn one lunch time, Chuck paid his bill and went out the front door leaving his sunglasses on the front counter.

I overhead Louise, the hostess, say, "He's done it again, and this time they're Oakley's."

The young pretty new girl walked up to the counter to look at them, "Yes, they're Oakley Batwolf's worth at least $200.

I sure wish I had these for my boyfriend back home."

Louise said, "They're yours kid, he'll never come back for them or ask about them."

The cute blonde put them in her bag under the counter exclaiming how much Ted would like them.

Chuck is tall and lanky and looks like he must have a gym up there in his penthouse. He lives in one of the many new high rise condo complexes which line the Gulf side of the Island. His penthouse has to be worth a lot of money.

Chuck doesn't seem to have a car of his own, but drives Launie's Cadillac as if it were his own. He docks the *Lollipop* all the way over in Pensacola, it's said, because no one closer will rent him a slip. When he comes back to pick up Launie he comes down the Sound and pulls up to the little pier that belongs to the Dorm.

Chuck is a mystery and people talk about how he can live as he does and not do anything but chauffer Launie. Libby Morat said she saw him riding his bike out on Highway 98 in the bike lane headed toward Destin. He either has a rooftop deck or goes to the beach because he has a great tan. He has a gym up there too, if his physique is any indication; he's not muscled out, but he's 'buff' as the kids would say. I'm six feet tall, and he is at least three inches taller. He stays out of trouble, seems to have few or no friends, and is seldom seen anywhere around the Island except at Tides Inn, or in either Fort Walton Beach or Destin.

I suppose since I have paid attention to him that others surely notice him too. The big mystery about Chuck is how does he get so much money, or maybe, how did he get it.

17
My Name is Ollie

The hard board of the bench behind the screen which was to keep him awake dug into his muscular thighs. His whole rear end felt like it was asleep.

The *ka-bang, ka-bang, ka-boom* of the drums grated in his head. He remembered another music, a music he loved….

"Spunk!"

"Spunk! You hear me? You get your sneakin skinny ass away from there. I can see you through that keyhole. I'm gonna pound you good! You hear me?"

He jumped back from the keyhole he was looking through and ran back down the hall as quick as his four-year-old legs would take him to his bed in the closet under a stairway. He had lived there all his life and didn't even know his real name.

"Blow!"

"It has five candles, Winnie! Am I five now?"

I'm not allowed to cry ever. Evelyn has the biggest tits of them all. My door is locked from the inside. I play with my toys the 'johns' bring me. Tits look like more fun.

Winnie put thirteen candles on this time.

His thighs clenched together and he felt the muscles in them stand out. His toes curled over the end of his bed that was too short now. He moved his hand up and down faster and faster and felt that unbelievable feeling start. His body jerked three, four, five times and he let out his breath. When his breathing was normal, he got up and threw the sticky hand towel in the hamper at the end of the hall where he had thrown so many like it. Nobody seemed to notice. He understood the smell he had smelled all his life: the place reeked of it.

Winnie cleaned out the 'cribs' every day. She was really the only one who had paid any attention to him. She would shake her head and he could hear her mutter, "Honey, no kid should live in a place like this."

"Run, Spunk! Run!"

He ran down the street to the big park that has the arch that lights up at night. He marched in step with the bronze statues that have horns and tambourines and trombones and trumpets and then ran around and around the whole procession pretending to be the leader jabbing a pretend baton up and down.

He heard the music of that band swaying down the street to a funeral—the swaying of the leader with his fancy hat and the mournful wail of the instruments. He had the hat! He led the dirge as they marched along but above it all he heard the trumpet—Satchmo's trumpet.

He ran to the part of the park he liked best because that was where all the dancing and music was. He found the people he liked there; Winnie's people and Creoles and Cubans and nearly whites like himself. Congo Square!

But I sit in my favorite place at the edge of the pond. I throw bread to the ducks. Pops Armstrong, the baddest dude of them all, stares at me blindly from his big statue.

Those kids are always passing by with backpacks full of books.

"Why you ain't goin to school? Mitch asked him.

"I'm not nobody. I got no name and they don't even know I'm here."

"That ain't no excuse. You know how to read?"

"No, suh."

"Well, I'm goin to learn you to read."

Mitch pulled out that old tattered book that had a little boy, a little girl, and a little spotted dog on the front of it. Who the hell was Mitch? What was he, an old white man, doing here in Spunk's park?

Spunk read the words, "See Spot? See Spot run?"

He went anywhere he wanted now and knew everybody in the Old Storyville district. Not too many people called the area that anymore, but the old timers did, and they were the ones Spunk listened to. He found out if he went to the back door of almost any joint, bar, or café in the area he could get enough food to last the whole day.

The streetcar lurched around a corner and he bounced in the seat as it rumbled over some ancient Live Oak roots. He rode all the way over to Prytania Street and saw a movie.

The Prytania Theater showed classic movies, had only one screen, and was the trickiest one to sneak into. But after his third or fourth trip over there, the old man at the door just waved him on inside.

The Green Arrow! He sat through it seven times, and when he left the theater, he would forever be known as Ollie, named by himself after Oliver Queen who played the Green Arrow.

Who the fuck is this Katrina bitch? Why was everybody talking about her? Somebody said she was out in the Gulf and headed toward the city. Gonna make a grand entrance, I guess. Fucked up Diva!

He awoke in the movie theater as huge guns shot their Nazi shells out across the Channel and realized the old theater was shaking in another wind.

The old man was not in the little lobby; fact was no one was in the theater except him. He grabbed a bag of popcorn as he ran through the front door. The howling wind grabbed it and the kernels looked like specks of fire as they shot through the air. By the time he was on the street, water was almost to his ankles.

Trouble Ollie, trouble...

Gotta get to 10. Long ways to 10, but 10 will be high up off the ground.

He passed Lil Dizzy's.

"Lots of food in there. Just sittin there to be taken," somebody running by him yelled.

He whirled around and enter the front door—first time he ever did that.

Ollie stuffed the backpack Mitch had given him which he always wore cause it had all his possessions in it, with pork chops, catfish, collard greens cooked almost to mush, and Dizzy's famous fried chicken. Grease covered Dick and Jane but he didn't see it. He grabbed a quart container of gumbo as he went out the door.

Running along Esplanade as fast as he could in the ankle deep water, he reached a high place where there was no water on the street and as he turned a corner around a big building, he came face to face with them. They must have been stranded on the high place for some time for they snarled, raised their heads in the air, bared their teeth, and charged at him as they smelled the food.

He hit the Pit Bull right between its eyes with the quart of gumbo. It burst open and the Pit Bull was not in the chase anymore.

He ran back as fast as he could with the heavy load and as he reached a fire escape ladder that had been pulled to the ground, he jumped up grabbing it with one arm while desperately holding on. The High Yellow leaped at him at the same time and ripped a gash in his left calf. Ollie yelled in pain, felt a fear he had never known, and scrambled up until he was at the top of the six story building.

He turned to look down and past the snarling dogs he saw a huge wave of water rolling down almost every street at him. He struggled, threw himself over the parapet that encircled the roof, and landed at Launie's feet.

"Ollie! Ollie, wake up! Damn it, you're sleeping again."

He felt the sharp pain in his calf and jerked upright on the stool. Kitty, one of Launie's girls, kicked him again with her high wedged heels. She was standing there holding out a Styrofoam container from Tides Inn. Ollie smelled the fish.

When Katrina caused the move to Fort Walton Beach, Launie couldn't just leave Ollie behind. She had seen him in the streets of New Orleans before and knew who he was when he landed at her feet. They had been on that building for three days and nights and the food in Ollie's backpack had been all thirteen of them had to eat until the helicopter pilot had finally seen them.

Ollie's job is to act as a deterrent to any trouble which might happen inside the strip joint; the bouncer. He sits on the high stool behind a screen in a back corner of the big room and appears to be in some other world. But, if a customer becomes rowdy or too complaining about something, he feels Ollie's big hand on his shoulder as he is guided to the exit.

When they can persuade him to come out from behind the screen, the girls take beer cans to Ollie for him to smash. The customers get a kick out it too. He doesn't play the game of smashing it against his head, even though that would not have hurt him, but he cups the can in his hand putting the bottom in his palm and wrapping his fingers around the top. He doesn't seem to exert any energy as the can flattens to a thin disk in his palm. Hundreds of the flattened cans are tacked along the top of the mirror behind the bar. The customers always ask what they are, and then turn to gaze at the screen. Most nights Ollie never leaves his stool, and not too many locals have ever seen him.

The Dorm is a remarkable building because it has stood through at least three hurricanes. Originally it had been a beautiful summer home on the Sound which belonged to a large family from Atlanta. The kids had begged for a place to bring their pet rabbits with them, so a rabbit hutch had been constructed behind the big house. The doctor's wife spent money with abandon on all the projects she undertook, so the hutch was really a two room building—one for the bucks and one for the does.

When Launie moved in, she built a bathroom adjacent to one of the rooms, and the little building became Ollie's home.

Ollie's one interest in life is to shoot his bow and arrows.

His Carbon Express Intercept crossbow which cost him over a $1000 is his prized possession. He found out one day it would shoot one of his steel-tipped arrows through the metal hull of an old abandoned boat.

Even Ollie realizes he is obsessed with the Green Arrow. One night as he was watching his TV in his little room, he happened across the new Arrow series and now each Wednesday night he disappears for an hour. Everyone knows to not bother him.

He had begged and pleaded with Launie for days until she gave in and built an enclosure behind his little house. It looks like a baseball bullpen from the outside except the walls are so high no one can see over them and the thuds of the arrows he shoots into the target sound like baseballs hitting a glove to anyone passing by.

Launie pays Ollie once a week in cash and he waits anxiously each week for his money so he can order more archery equipment on Amazon.

One of the girls, Ester, who Ollie talks with more than any other person takes his cash to Security Bank and deposits it for him. He is astounded that he only has to put in some numbers and push enter and then he marvels when a box arrives with his name on it. It is like something fell out of the sky to him. Launie might have shown more interest if she had known the arsenal Ollie is accumulating.

Launie thought from the beginning that Ollie was almost retarded and would be easy to control if she offered him the right things. She soon found out that Ollie really isn't retarded; he's just antisocial. He just wants to be alone. When he discovered her laptop, she was truly surprised how quickly he learned how to work it. He spends hours now on his own computer in his little room admiring his one interest in life, Oliver Queen and his adventures.

The girls take care of Ollie like he is their protective brother. Since Launie believes none of the local folks know about Ollie, they bring all his food in for him. During the eight years Launie has been in Fort Walton, Ollie hasn't been out on the street.

At least that's what Launie believes, but she doesn't know his secret place down in the vacant space where no houses have been built along the Sound; a place left vacant so that storm waters have a ditch to drain into the Sound. Ollie slips out, usually in the night time after Launie's closes, and goes to his 'fort,' a cave he has dug high on the bank of one of those channels.

18

Max

Max hauled himself out of bed. He realized he was naked as he headed to the bathroom. He knew he shouldn't have had so much to drink last night; Red Bull and Vodka. When the first pangs of the headache hit him, he stumbled.

He thought what the heck is that horrible smell? It smelled like apricots which always made him sick to his stomach. It seemed his whole room was filled with it.

He smelled his arm and it stunk with it. He stood in front of the commode and would have made a race horse proud with the stream he pissed. He tore open the shower curtain, turned the shower on full blast, and stood as the cold water woke him. He scrubbed and scrubbed to get that wickedly sweet smell off his body; it was like an oil of some kind. He had no idea what he had done last night nor where he had been. As he stood in his usual cold shower, he wondered how he got home and what had happened to his clothes.

He didn't want to go to work today. What a hellish place the La Mancha had become, he thought. Why wouldn't people leave him alone about that body? That was a real mess. She probably was good looking and she sure did have a nice body. He pictured the muscles in her legs and thought maybe she was a runner. Or maybe a swimmer?

When he got dressed, he couldn't find his car keys. After fifteen minutes of searching, he went down to his prized possession and the keys were in the ignition. Someone had scribbled "SUCKER!" across the windshield with bright red lipstick. He was furious at the lipstick but more so with himself for he never parked the Fairlane anywhere without putting the cover on it, much less leave the keys in it. What had happened last night to cause him to forget?

Max and his dad had driven all the way to Jefferson City, Missouri two summers ago to see, and ultimately buy the 1956 Ford coupe. It had been in really bad condition, but his dad had convinced him to spend over $7,000 for it. They had hauled it back on his dad's flatbed truck, and worked on it every chance they got. Now, it was his pride and joy. All the women turned and looked at him when he passed by in it. Now it was ivory white with a red half-top and the chrome strips which swooped down the front fenders, curved down on the door, and continued straight to the tail lights were shiny. His favorite thing was the futuristic hood ornament which was supposed to be some bird in flight but reminded him more of a sleek catamaran out on the Gulf.

He went back into his apartment, got some cleaner and a rag, and when he had completely erased the lipstick from the windshield, he headed down the twelve miles on Highway 98 through Fort Walton Beach. The sick smell filled his car which increased his anger, so he rode with all the windows down. The bitch must have been wearing a bottle of it. He grumbled as he wondered how long it would take to get rid of it.

As he passed the produce stand, he thought he wanted a peach, so he made a U turn and went back the west bound lane, made another U turn and pulled into the lot. He knows Freddie who runs the place because he stops several times a week to get some fruit on his way to work, and as he picked out a peach, he saw the machete hanging above the counter window, "Been hacking any banana bunches, lately?"

"Two this week," Freddie laughed.

As Max went on through Fort Walton Beach, crossed Brooks Bridge which goes over the Sound and connects the Island with the mainland, he thought that guy sure doesn't talk much. At the end of the

63

bridge he turned into the gas station for he saw the gas tank was nearly empty. He walked in to put a twenty on the counter.

As most twenty years olds do, he paid cash. His wallet was empty. Damn, he had over three hundred dollars yesterday afternoon. He left without buying any gas, and realized he was in trouble for money for the rest of the week.

That's what the 'SUCKER' was for on his windshield he realized as he slammed his fist down on the steering wheel. He sure as hell better not find out who the bitch was.

He turned right and started up Santa Rosa Blvd toward the La Mancha. He almost stopped at the Tom Thumb to see his woman, but she hadn't talked to him in days, and besides he didn't have any money to burn on Gator Ade, so he went on by.

He told himself he didn't care, but he did. He wondered why he loved women so much, any woman. She didn't have to be beautiful nor his age. He just loved women. He also knew he was attractive, but that's not why most women liked him after getting to know him. He was polite and attentive to the one he was with, and that's why so many of them gave him big tips at the beach. Well, he would need those big tips this week, for damn sure.

He pulled into the La Mancha and wished he hadn't.

Morat was still holding court at the pool, and motioned Max to come over.

Morat stuffed a chocolate kiss into his mouth and the foil went flying into the pool as he said, "Sit down over there and wait till I finish with Mrs. Thompson."

"I'm already late for work, and my boss will not like it."

"Just sit."

Max sat down in a pool chair about as far as he could get from Morat's table. He had that headache and his stomach had not liked that peach. He felt like a fool that some two-bit hussy had suckered him for $300. He knew where to look for her he thought, and there would be hell to pay when he found her.

Mrs. Thompson lived on the first floor of Pelican, Max knew. He didn't pay much attention to what Morat was asking her. He didn't really care.

She finally got up to leave saying, "Yes! Yes, Detective Morat, I will certainly let you know if I hear or learn anything!"

Morat beamed at her for she had emphasized

"Detective" and then beckoned for Max to join him.

"Why did you lie to me about what time you got to work that morning?"

Max hesitated just a little too long, but said, "Cause I was late."

"You mean because you were coming back the second time, don't you?"

"What are you talking about? I was just getting here. I stopped to get a Gator Ade."

"At the Tom Thumb?"

"Yes."

"You stop there an awful lot, don't you?"

"If you had to sit down here on the beach in the heat, you would get away every once in a while, and go get something to drink. Daniel knows I do it."

"Yes, he does. I talked to him."

"He's going to have my butt if I don't get the beach set up this morning. Look, sir, I was somewhere I shouldn't have been talking to someone who is having problems, and I was late. Now, may I go to work? Oh, by the way, Daniel was down on the beach that morning before any of us."

Suddenly Max had Morat's attention, "What do you mean? How do you know? Why didn't you tell me this before now/"

"You never ask me."

Morat spluttered, "You know bloody well that I am trying to find out how that woman died, and you keep information to yourself? I'll have your butt in jail, young man. Now, how do you know Daniel was down on the beach that morning?"

"He left me a note under a piece of drift wood on top the big box that holds the chairs and umbrellas. It said he took a kayak out really early that morning. He does it all the time— likes to get the exercise while it's still cool."

"What time did he get back?"

"I certainly wouldn't know. You, yourself, accused me of coming back for the second time. I was late, you remember?"

Morat turned bright red and almost shouted, "Just go on the work. I'll talk to Daniel myself."

Max had a big grin on his face as he went down the ramp from the gazebo to the sand. He had evened the score with Morat, he thought. He also knew that Daniel had taken the kayak down to another condo complex where they had the beach business.

Morat shook his head as Max walked away; he popped another chocolate kiss into his mouth.

19

Morat, at His Wit's End

Morat had been asked to move his interrogation table away from the pool because the guests wouldn't come down and use it while he was there and the grounds crew was complaining about all the pieces of foil on the deck and in the pool.

He was at his wit's end. He had no idea how that body had washed up on the shore or any clue as to who had cut off her hands, and most of all, who she was. He knew his interviews were useless for whoever had done this thing could be a thousand miles away and completely anonymous. He suspected everyone. He sat in the gazebo, where he had taken up residence, and look out over the Gulf.

He grumbled as he saw a piece of foil float to the floor from his pants leg and he had to pick it up. His agreement was he would use the trash can or he could take his interviews to his office at City Hall. When he sat back down, he landed on a little piece of chocolate which would make a conspicuous stain exactly in the wrong place on the white poly pants every time he stood.

Blevins came walking down the boardwalk and sat down on the bench next to Morat. "You know it's impossible to know where that boat goes… We have the records of when it leaves the slip at Pensacola and when it comes back, but you can write anything down as to where you are going…

He paused because he wasn't sure Morat was listening.

"Chuck Jenkins has no record at all. He's a clean-cut guy who is a loner and who has a lot of money. Who knows where he gets it or how he got it... Launie probably pays him well, but not enough for him to be living like he does. But, then again, he doesn't have a car, so really all he spends is on that condo and clothes. Launie buys all his food for him...wonder what the real connection is between the two of them."

Morat who had had his eyes closed, looked up because he had been resting his chin on his chest and said, "Drugs?"

"Nothing that we know about, but that boat sure would be a way to pick them up."

"Can he be followed?"

"Oh, come on Detective! If we were to follow him out there in that open water, don't you think he would see us?"

Morat glared at him, "Yeah... But maybe that's what happened the other morning when he was seen speeding away."

20

A Mystery with Money

Josephine Jones moved into Condo 62 in Dolphin building about two years ago. Told us she was from Europe. Sweden, I think. That wasn't her real name, but no one knew that then. She had paid cash for the top floor condo, and I saw her most mornings as she sat on her balcony with her binoculars. She, too, was a student of the Gulf, I thought. Occasionally, I would wave at her, and maybe get a wave back, but most times she was too engrossed in scanning the horizon.

I was one of the few full-time residents who would speak to her. She kept to herself, walked Skipper, her Corgi, every morning, met and passed Walkin Al without saying a word of greeting, and would return to her condo. Brantley especially dislike her for she never picked-up Skipper's messes.

Josephine was really not a likable person. She is one of the most attractive women I have encountered in my many years, tall and very athletic. She has a figure that most women would be envious of and which lots of men stop to admire. She runs the trail out alongside Santa Rosa Blvd most mornings; the three plus mile run doesn't seem to make her break a sweat. She swims in the Gulf as easily as the dolphins do, racing down the beach from the gazebo, gracefully diving into the water, and heading east all the way to Anglers Pier about two miles away with steady rhythmic strokes. She gets out of the water there and runs back on the beach in her wet swim suit; this is her morning routine if she isn't running the Blvd.

But, when she opens her mouth, everything changes. She is really foul-mouthed and cusses like a sailor. When she goes to the pool, the permanent residents make of point of having to go in as they have forgotten to do something, and the tourists soon wish they had also. Every other word would make a rapper blush.

And she passes gas—really loud farts that usually really stink. She laughs loudly and always says, "How bout that?"

None of us know anything about her. She doesn't work, but seems to have money for anything she wants. She wears a huge blue Safire on her right hand set in platinum and surrounded with diamonds. She has a different car each year, and they all seem to be last year's model. And they all looked familiar to me, but I couldn't pin it down, and I didn't really care.

I was out walking along the trail on the Blvd one morning and happened to see her up ahead of me. She wasn't running, but walking as I was. She paused across the street from one of the larger condo buildings and stood looking up at it, really inspecting it, until I almost caught up with her. She started walking again and then broke into running with those long strides of hers.

I saw her go to the stop light at the end of the Blvd, stand running in place until the crossing light turned green at 98 and she could take off again, and then head around the curve in the street toward Launie's. I walked on down to the Tom Thumb, bought a frozen fruit bar and ate it on the way back to the La Mancha.

Josephine passed me long before I got back to the La Mancha gate. As she passed me, she let out a husky outrageous laugh, and I heard, "How bout that?"

21
Nellie

Just like Scout, Jem, and Dill had Mrs. Henry Lafayette Dubose, all small towns seem to have that one old lady who knows everything that is happening, everybody's business, and tries to control the young people of the town. At least, they all think they do! Even though the La Mancha complex bumps against more condo complexes on the east side, it's really like a little community to itself. And we have our Mrs. Dubose in one Nellie Tromley. She lives in Seagull on the second floor where the building curves creating two units which have much larger balconies. Condo 24 is almost directly below Paul Bishop and his mom.

She seems to be infected with that disease all the other ones I have known or read about, "I-itis." Every sentence begins with 'I' and 'I' is used at least two times in the sentence, but probably several times more. Every cure is one that only 'I' can offer. Every accusation is 'I' won't have this, and 'I' will see that you get into trouble. Nellie is a pro.

She has few friends and if she ever comes to a social function, most people quickly abandon her. She never seems to notice. She can't be much over five feet tall and undoubtedly weighs much less than a hundred pounds, but her voice is much larger as it cuts across a room or from her balcony in its shrill tones.

She yells at Brantley when he is picking up trash each morning saying it's none of his darn concern and that 'I' have a yard crew to take care of the lawns. One of her pet peeves is seeing some young person riding a skateboard on one of the walks. "I see you can't you read, you little piss ant. There's a sign posted by the front gate that there will be no skateboarding on this property! So you just get off that dang thing and carry it! You hear me? I'll call security!

I heard her clear over from my balcony yelling at a tourist who was feeding bread to some seagulls. "Those damn birds spread disease, and I live here and I don't need them up around my building. They poop all over the place! So, you just stop, you hear me?"

Unlike Mrs. Dubose in *To Kill a Mocking Bird*, Nellie is not confined to a wheel chair, but she might have been better off if she had been. One evening she was walking along the walk by the front entrance and saw a complete stranger give Gerald some money. Gerald stuck it in his pocket and allowed the young woman to enter the property. Nellie watched the whole transaction and then saw the woman go up the parking lot toward Dolphin building. She decided then and there that she did not like Gerald and never had liked him. She would report this to Bicycle Bob who is the president of the Owner's Association.

But Nellie made a decision which would land her in the hospital with a broken nose for over two weeks as she followed the young woman and saw her get on the elevator in Dolphin.

Nellie stood in front of the two elevator doors waiting for the woman to come back down from the 6th floor. Nellie had seen on the light above the doors and knew where the young woman had gone. As the elevator was descending, Nellie stationed herself right in front of the door. As the door opened, Nellie confronted her in all her wrath, "What are you doing here? I know you do not belong on the property and furthermore I want to see some identification."

The young woman replied, "Who do you think you are?"

"I live here and I take it as my responsibility to see that things are right."

"Get out of my way, old woman, or you will get hurt!"

Nellie hesitated in disbelief, turned a bright red and hissed at the girl, "I'll call Security!"

"You just do that, and I'll just give him more money.

Now, get out of my way."

As the woman tried to get past her, Nellie stepped to block her way. The woman swung the big heavy purse she was carrying and hit Nellie squarely in the face. Nellie was thrown backward and hit her head on the metal frame of the elevator door as she fell.

The young woman hurried off as fast as she could. She knew if she went through the back pole-gate, she would be off the property much quicker than going back through the front. As she ran toward the gate, she saw a shiny yellow Porsche which she knew belonged to Brantley.

Josephine had heard the yelling as she closed her condo door. She was taking Skipper out for his nightly walk. She hurried to the elevator, got to the ground floor, and found Nellie. She called 911 on her cell phone, and a few minutes later the ambulance went wailing down the Blvd taking Nellie to the emergency room.

Since Nellie returned to her condo several days later, she hasn't been down on the walks. She sits in a low chair on her balcony, with her black eyes and broken nose, hiding behind the railing thinking, I suppose, that no one can see her, but she can still see everything that happens. She drinks rum and Coke, throws the bottles off her balcony, and curses everything about the La Mancha.

She was furious when Betty, the La Mancha manager, didn't even talk to Gerald about the young woman or the money. "Probably one of the damn hookers from that strip joint up across 98. Damn White trash come in here from New Orleans," she had yelled at Betty as she slammed down the receiver on her old-fashioned phone.

22

Ryan's Day Off

Ryan stood in front of the dusty mirror and inspected himself. He had on one of his best shirts and a pair of those jeans that have the shiny stripes down each leg. He really didn't understand fashion, but it seemed everyone was wearing them, and that blonde at Tides Inn had noticed them. He tried to persuade himself he was going to Tides Inn for a free beer and a half dozen oysters because they would think he'd done a good job this week, but he knew exactly why he was going. Besides, Brantley was out on a stinking oil rig somewhere and he wouldn't be hanging around to get into the conversation—if there was a conversation.

Sometimes Ryan wondered just how he and Brantley started hanging out together. He remembered when Brantley first started being everywhere he was and he had thought it was strange. He would walk around the corner to his locker on his way to the next class at FWBH and Brantley would be standing a few feet from his locker. He noticed Brantley had been transferred into two of his classes well into the semester. Then he found out how smart Brantley was with class work, and Ryan accepted him. Ryan's grades improved a lot and things were much better for him at home with his mom.

He drove his old Chevy pickup up the unpaved lane alongside the landing strip, waved at his buddy Freddie who helped him with the banners, and pulled out onto Highway 98.

Since high school eight years ago, he had bounced around from job to job until one of his uncles had loaned him the money to buy his plane. His uncle had taught him how to fly and he earned his pilot's license by the time he was eighteen while he was still in school. They had flown all the way to Arizona and driven up to Sedona where they found the Waco, a 2007 model with few air miles on it. Flying all the way back to the little landing strip by the Sound had been quite an adventure. His uncle had the banner business, but had grown tired of it and had sold Ryan the plane and his business. He still owed too much money to his uncle, but he was getting there.

Ryan lives by himself in a little house he rented which was on the Sound. About all he ever did was fish in the Gulf anywhere he could as often as he could, run around with Brantley, drink beer, and talk about women.

He didn't understand Brantley actually but they had been on the football team in high school together and just started hanging together once Brantley proved what help he was with grades. Ryan was the star wide receiver on FWBH's football team, but Brantley didn't play except for one down the whole season when the coach put him in during their last game when they were way ahead. Ryan had a tremendous season his senior year and was a McDonald's All American. He was offered many scholarships in the SEC but none of them paid a full ride and he didn't have money to pay the rest.

Brantley always left right after the game or practice because his mom would be waiting for him. Ryan was never invited to his house even though his mom had invited Brantley to eat with them many times. Brantley had eaten with them twice, Ryan remembered, but his mom came and took him home right after dinner.

The two of them seldom did more than hang out on an afternoon at Tides Inn together, and once they had gone to Launie's. Ryan blushed every time he thought about that.

As he pulled into Tides Inn, he noticed they were not very busy today, so darn his luck, she probably wouldn't be there. He was right. The guy who shucks oysters behind the bar said she just didn't come in to work a few days ago and no one could get a hold of her. He guessed she was homesick and had gone back to Mississippi or wherever it was.

Ryan seldom or never cussed, but he said a dirty word under his breath. He drank a free beer and ate a dozen free oysters, got into his car and headed back home. He didn't have anything today, so he thought he might go fishing as he knew the Red Snapper were running.

23

A Dangerous Discovery, A
Wonderful Realization

Paul helped his mother by working at any job he could find. Trish made good money running one of the rental agencies that rents condos to the tourists but Paul wanted to earn his own money to help out. He saw Josephine's Caddy and asked her if he could keep it looking its best for her. She was glad to have him do it, and appreciated it so much she allowed him to drive it from her building to behind Seashell building where Marvin had allowed him to set-up his car washing business.

He saw some other fine local cars, and soon he had more than fifteen he was washing and shining whenever he could. He saw Chuck Jenkins one day at Tides Inn and hit him up about keeping the car Chuck drove in good shape. Chuck was pleased, and about once a week, Paul would walk or run down to where Chuck lived in his penthouse, go up to the seventh floor, ring the bell, and Chuck would hand him the key without really opening the door very far.

That Saturday morning when Paul walked up the Blvd toward Chuck's condo, his muscles were sore from the night before and occasionally he would stop and stretch them. The night before several of Paul's friends had challenged each other to a mini-iron man contest. They started in front of the gazebo and swam the two miles down to Angler's Pier to the east, got out and ran back on the beach and then rode their boards out and around where they had anchored a make-shift buoy.

Roche had easily won the swim leg since she is the reigning long distant swimmer in the State, but Paul was close behind. The run back to the La Mancha was a race between Paul and his friend Sam who runs Cross Country for FWBH, but when they mounted their boards, Paul pulled his board out to the buoy with such speed that he left Doogs, Roche, and all the far behind. He waved to them as he headed back to shore.

As he was driving back toward the La Mancha, he saw Roche, up ahead of him in her 1986 bright red Volkswagen Bug. He loved that car, and suddenly he thought he just might also love the driver. He pulled up close behind her and tapped the horn. She retaliated by almost stopping in front of him, and drove under five miles per hour weaving back and forth down the lane until they reached the guard shack at the La Mancha. She didn't even stop as Gerald waved her past but headed straight down toward the parking area at the beach. Paul really wanted to go after her, but he had to get Chuck's car back in an hour.

He knew he couldn't skimp on the brand new Cadillac or he might lose Chuck as a customer, and nobody tipped like Chuck. He had washed and polished the outside and was now inside the big new-smelling car. He finished the hard part; the area of the front seat and the dash. He got out, opened the back door, and crawled in to clean the back window, the back seats, and the floor.

He was cleaning the floor, the last thing to be done, and then he could join Roche, but as he reached under the front seat he felt a plastic bag. He pulled it out and saw it was one of those zip bags. It was filled till it ballooned with a white powder. He knew instantly what it was. What was he going to do with it, he thought.

But destiny or something has a way of interfering for his cell phone rang. He heard the crash of the waves on the beach as Roche sang a little of the song both of them called theirs at the present time.

He was running late and had to get the Caddy back to Chuck, and Roche was down there in a two piece and he wanted to be there. The zip bag fell into a bucket he used to scrub tires, and Paul drove off down the Blvd to take Chuck's car back. He really wasn't thinking of anything except to get back to his condo, change into his trunks, and hit the beach where she waited for him.

Roche was floating on a board fifty or so feet from the shore, Paul dove into the first good wave he saw and came up under the board, stood and raised it out of the water dumping her into shallow water. She came up spluttering and that twinkle in her bright brown eyes said clearly, "You better watch out, Dude!"

She had both arms wrapped around his ankles before he knew what happened, and as she pulled back he flopped into the water slapping his back with a loud bang. He winched at the sting, and called time out.

The rest of the afternoon they lay in the sun talking about what they would like to do in the future. She wanted to go abroad and see Italy, and Paul knew her dad who was President of a local bank could afford to send her. She loved art and wanted to spend weeks in Florence.

She turned to him and said, "But I have my David right here."

He turned red, jumped up and was in a big incoming wave as he heard her laugh.

When he got out, he said, "Come on, I want to show you something."

They walked up the ramp to the gazebo and up the boardwalk to the sidewalk, turned right and a few steps later, he walked over and sat down on the wall looking out toward the water he loved so much. He beckoned her over and as they sat there, he pointed out the seagull sitting on top the volleyball goal post, "His name is Jonathan L. and he's a guy who knows he has to take care of himself. I sit here and wonder what will happen to me and who will be in my life, and I think you should think of that too. Because you might just be a part of it, if you want…."

"You are one silly guy, you know that? I have known for months that I am a part of your life and you a part of mine, and I think I just might like that! Forever...."

He leaned over, put his hand behind her head, pulled her to him and kissed her softly on the lips. They broke apart, smiled at each other, and the second kiss was not soft and not short.

Jonathan squawked and flew away!

24

Morat Jumps to Conclusions

I didn't go down to the beach again this morning. Yesterday morning was a disaster as several people have seen me with Morat and stopped me asking all the questions I wouldn't answer. The La Mancha is not a very pleasant place to be right now.

Even Jonathan L seems upset. I will see him jump into the air like only seagulls do, dive toward the gazebo where Morat is, fly a loop over and around the pool and return to the volleyball goal post. It occurred to me, where does Jonathan eat?

Seven of us went over to Destin last night to get away from this place and get some good food at El Pinto. It has to be the best Mexican food around, except it really isn't Mexican. It's a cross between what I've always eaten in Albuquerque and Mexican. They use New Mexican chilies in everything which makes it like 'home' to me. We ate in the bar and had maybe one too many of Russ's fine margaritas.

I drove and therefore had only one margarita, and as we came back on the Island, I saw Max's Fairlane turn down the street toward Launie's. I didn't say anything to the others in my car, but why in the world would a good-looking rugged twenty-three-year old be going to a place like that? I almost slapped myself up the side of the head…Yeah, what would a red blooded twenty-three-year old be doing there…Right!

I have lost track of days. I tried to go about my routine of getting the Cuisinart coffee machine ready, then walk out into the dark morning breeze, and do my walking on the beach. But things are different now. I have lost my drive, and the walks are becoming shorter and shorter. I sit out on the balcony more in the evenings after dark. I sit and try to think because I feel I have forgotten something.

Tonight as I sit here, a plane flies over. It's one of the little twenty passenger jets that lands at Valparaiso, but it reminded me of a night before the body was found. I had heard a plane that night, but it was not a jet. It sounded like that little plane that pulls those advertising banners and it sounded like it was having some kind of trouble. I had pictured it, I remember thinking, as pitching back and forth and sputtering. One time it roared as the pilot must have really sped up after one of those sputtering times. I could kick myself for forgetting about it. It was too late, or maybe I should say too early, to call Morat so I will wait until morning.

I didn't sleep much.

His phone rang too many times and I was getting ready to hang up when a female voice came on. It was Elsie, the dispatcher. My call had been switched to her line. Heaven help me get through this with her I thought.

I said very slowly, "May I speak to Detective Morat?"

"Who is speaking," she asked.

"I live at the La Mancha and I was the one who called you to send the deputies out here the other day."

Saying that was a horrible mistake.

"Oh, Dear! Oh, Dear! We don't have another body, do we? We've never had anything like this before! Oh, Dear!

"No!" I shouted. "I just need to talk to Detective Morat."

"He isn't here yet. Do you want me to call the deputies?

I know they're over in Destin this morning."

83

"No!" I shouted. "I don't want the deputies."

I almost laughed. How in that world did they ever get anything done at that place?

"I'll call back."

"No, wait, here he comes."

I heard her say to Morat, "Oh, Dear Me! Detective Morat, there's more trouble out at the La Mancha."

I shuddered, but Morat came on the phone.

"Morat, here, who's on the line?"

I told him and said I had something I thought he would want to know. He said he was coming out anyway, so I could wait and tell him in person.

It took him longer than it should have, and I would wager he stopped at the Tom Thumb and bought his day's supply of those little kisses.

This was the first time Morat had actually come up to my condo. He went straight out to the balcony after grunting something sounding like 'hello,' and sat down in one of the two high pub chairs I have there.

"I wondered how you saw so much from up here, but I understand now. What a view… I also see you can't see where she was. I actually didn't believe you and that's why I was coming out here this morning. Now, what is it you want to tell me?"

"I was out here thinking last night because something was just not right about what happened that night before we found her. Then, one of the passenger jets flew over, and I remembered that I had heard a plane that night. I am almost certain it was that same little plane that pulls the banners."

Morat actually cussed at me in French, I think, and pushed me toward the door. "Hurry! Go down and get in my car. You're going with me and you're going to go over everything you can remember as we go out to that little airstrip."

He turned on the siren, naturally, and we went down the Blvd at over 60, over Brooks Bridge at least 50, and through Fort Walton Beach faster than I thought possible. The tourist cars scattered in front of us and I thought he was going straight through the produce stand when we left Highway 98. Freddie was actually scared for his life as he jumped out of the way, and it took him a long minute to blurt out that Ryan was already out on a trip with a banner.

Morat cussed again, I think, and we sped done the lane toward Ryan's house. I thought the man would have a stroke before I heard the little plane coming in to change banners. I had seen the frustration that had built up in Morat over the last few days, and now the relief when the plane had landed.

He arrested Ryan, handcuffed him, and read him his rights. Ryan hadn't even protested as I saw he was nearly laughing out loud at Morat.

We headed back up the lane to 98 and saw Freddie standing in the middle of the lane waving his hand for us to stop. He held a machete in his other hand. I thought Morat was going to have a seizure as he struggled to get his gun out of the glove compartment of the car. He brought the car to a stop right in front of Freddie and aimed his revolver at him.

"Wait! Wait! Freddie almost screamed. "I just want to show you what I found."

Ryan spoke up from behind the mesh screen in the back seat, "For cryin out loud, it's just Freddie."

Morat glared in Ryan's direction as he got out of the car, "Put that weapon down, young man or you'll be in cuffs too."

Freddie had never seen Morat before, I'm guessing, "But, sir, I just noticed what's on this a few minutes ago. It's got nicks on it and what looks like blood."

Morat stopped, "Just lay it on the ground and step back. Prof, can you use that radio?

"I have no idea how," I answered.

Morat turned red, "Where is Blevins when I need him?" I almost laughed, but didn't.

"Get on your knees and hold the back of your head with your hands, young man. And know I will have this gun on you the whole time." He inched back toward the car, took two or three tries to get the radio mike cord through the window and finally reached Blevins.

Blevins arrived ten long minutes later, questioned Freddie, and took the machete as evidence.

Ryan was out of jail in a few hours after he proved he was in Panama City the night of the murder. He told Morat about his suspicions about his plane's fuel and the funny smell that he continued to smell. Morat asked who else could have flown his plane, and Ryan hesitated a long time before he would answer. Morat was furious. Then he told Morat that Brantley knew where a set of keys were.

Morat whirled around at me, "How often does he go out there? How long does he stay?"

"Detective, I don't know the answer to either of those questions really, but sometimes it seems he's gone for weeks. I don't know where he has been though."

Morat glared at me and walked away. Blevins walked beside him and I could hear Blevins say they would have a hard time getting Brantley off the rigs out there.

25

Brantley on His Own

Two nights before Max found the body on the beach, Brantley pulled up to Tides Inn in his Honda he thought no one knew about at the La Mancha. He kept it parked at a parking lot out on Air Port Road in Destin. He had a ticket on the windshield again tonight, so he knew he would have to move it to another place. He really didn't understand why he wanted to keep it a secret, but he did.

Brantley did things like that.

He knew Ryan was away in Panama City and he would have all the attention from that pretty new waitress at Tides Inn. He looked at himself in the mirror as he entered the entryway of the bar. He looked his best. She was waiting on a table back near the old buoy marker sign which they have made into a dart board. He didn't have to tell Louise, the perky woman who seats people where he wanted to sit; she just led him straight to the blonde's section.

He sat down, nervously turning the menu over as it was upside down as it always was from Louise. He thought she did it only to him to get a laugh from Marvin's brother who works behind the bar. The blonde approached carrying a glass of water with lemon in it as he liked, and he saw with satisfaction she had been there long enough for her nametag to have arrived. "Caroline" it read. Man, that fit her to a tee, he thought. She looked like a Caroline. She looked so innocent and clean.

He stammered that he wanted a beer and a dozen oysters when she asked him what he was having. He watched her walk away from him and quickly turned to see that Marvin's brother shucking oysters was grinning from ear to ear at him. Brantley frowned and lowered his face toward the table.

She brought the draft Bud and oysters and asked, "Will that be all tonight, Brantley?"

He thought he would choke when she said his name, and he could only shake his head as she left. He wondered if he would ever be able to talk with her.

He finished the beer and oysters, and saw as she approached with his ticket that a stranger had come in and sat down on a stool at the bar. She had been in the back and had not seen the guy.

She handed Brantley his ticket, and when she turned and saw the young man, she let out a little shriek, "Ted!" ran over and threw her arms around him and they kissed passionately right there in front of everyone. They stood under the old john boat that is decorated with string lights that hangs upside-down over the bar and kiss a long almost frantic kiss as everyone in the place applauded except Brantley who was red with anger.

Brantley thought he was going to be sick. He left a dollar on the table, went up front and paid his bill, and angrily strode out to the Honda. He sat there a while, cussing, and finally decided to go to Launie's.

26

Murder

The place reeks of stale smoke. The music is canned rap or disco or R&B and has a tinny sound except for the old man who sits at the back banging away on the drums. Most of the girls d0 their routine from the track music, but Brantley likes the looks of one of the girls, a blonde, of course, named Kitty who grinds and plays on a pole to the beat of the old drummer.

"Ka-boom, ka-boom, boom, boom," fills him with a desire he's never fulfilled.

He always sits at the table right in front of where she always dances. Only one of girls dance at a time and he always sits with his head lowered drinking beer until Kitty comes out. He gives her lots of tips and she pays particular attention to him.

Tonight he is so angry about what had happened at Tides Inn he made up his mind to talk to Kitty. He waits impatiently until she finishes her turn dancing for him and he is excited more than he ever has been. He turns and what he sees are a bunch of old men in the place, disgusting old men smoking and gazing at her. He is furious. He gazes at one in particular as he has seen that one walking around the La Mancha complex many times. He quickly looks away from him and follows Kitty toward the bar where the girls always go after they perform. Laurie had taught them well, for they flirt with the patrons at the bar and sell lots of beer--and get good tips.

He approached her and mumbled, "Hello."

She smiled at him and asked, "What can I do for you?"

"Er, you can come sit with me, if you want."

"Sure thing. What you got in mind big guy?

"Just need some company tonight."

"Sure thing! I'll get you a drink."

They sat and she talked and he had several beers as she paid complete attention to him. The bartender kept sending drinks and Kitty kept helping herself to the money in Brantley's wallet as she paid for them.

Then he was aware he was walking and someone was helping him. Somehow whoever it was knew he was in the old Honda, and he felt himself pushed into the passenger side seat. Whoever it was started the car and they left Launie's.

Brantley saw the familiar sights down the Blvd all run together in a blur as they went by them, and felt the car make the sharp left turn and then the right as it pulled up to the guard house at the La Mancha. The car just hesitated and then entered the complex. Brantley saw Gerald give his little salute to the driver.

What was that smell he loved so much? His mother had worn it… He breathed in deeply and it filled his senses.

How did whoever it was know where to go? Was he talking out loud? Had he talked about where he lived? Why wouldn't the person answer him for he asked two or three times?

He felt the car stop and his door was opened. Someone helped him out and guided him down the walk to his door. His keys were on the car key ring and he heard his front door open. He was helped into his bedroom and he fell on the bed.

When he awoke, he was on his bed and someone was in his room. Jasmine filled the whole room.

He was terrified. Was she back?

Then, he realized it was Kitty and that she was sitting in a chair watching him. He stood and she did to. She was nude. She walked to him and started unbuttoning his shirt.

She undid his belt and his pants dropped to the floor. She pull down his boxers. Suddenly Brantley remembered this happening before and he started crying.

"I'll not do it again Mommy! I'll remember to go potty in the potty… I'm sorry Mommy. Don't put me in the wardrobe."

Kitty stepped back startled. Then she looked at Brantley's body. He was completely without hair and when she looked down; she gasped and started to laugh.

Brantley was enraged. No one had ever seen him since he became a grown man. No one, except his mom. He saw the Japanese blades on the wall behind her and grabbed the nearest one. He swung it and as the heavy copper hilt came around it hit her squarely near the side of her nose. The ornate carvings cut into her cheek so he could see the white of her teeth as she fell onto the bed.

The blade also had slid along and sliced in the meaty part between his finger and thumb. He instinctively raised his hand to his mouth to stop the flow of blood and thought he had some of her blood on it also. He puked onto the sheet.

Brantley was horrified as he saw she was bleeding on his bed. He slapped her hard with his open hand. She didn't move. Then he realized she was dead. She would not laugh at him and she would not tell his secret.

Blood was splattered over the sheet. He saw that the cut was bleeding freely. Grabbing a towel from the bathroom, he wrapped it tightly around his hand.

Then Brantley was scared. What do I do, he thought?

How am I going to get away with this? He ran to the wardrobe, wrapped his arms around it as far as he could reach, and his blood leaked from the towel and ran down its side. He screamed his little kid scream again. He peed on himself and didn't care.

Suddenly he heard his mother's voice. She was telling him what to do. She had always had the answers for him. He listened and her plan slowly developed in his mind.

"Roll that filthy bitch in a quilt, drive out to Ryan's house, take Ryan's plane out over the Gulf and throw her out," his mom was telling him. "Throw her out!"

He knew Ryan was not in town and he knew where the keys to the plane were.

He found the stash of Piggly Wiggly sacks underneath the sink in the kitchen and pulled one over her head to catch the blood. It ballooned up like a globe and he realized that there were many bags stuffed into the one he had put over her head. She looked like something from space.

He and his mother laughed as he wrapped ribbon from his mother's sewing basket around and around the bags and tied them in a neat little bow. He stuck his hand into one of the bags and tie a knot using his mouth to tighten the bow. They both laughed again.

As he took a shower, he knew he would be flying out to one of the rigs in the morning and might not be back for days.

The bleeding had stopped; he wrapped his hand in a bandage, and convinced himself no one would suspect him of doing something like this.

"Use Pledge on the wardrobe, Brantley. You messed it up." He hurried to clean off the blood and his piss.

Getting the body outside and into his car was a terrifying event. He peered out his door for what seemed minutes. He saw that no one was about. Anyone could be out—Marvin was always out and about. That old teacher was always sitting on his balcony! But he didn't see anyone.

All the buildings at the La Mancha are brightly lit at night to show planes where they are, and to provide a secure place for the residents. "Unscrew the light bulb by the door, Brantley," his mother whispered. It took him several minutes to get the old-fashioned globe off the bulb and then he unscrewed the bulb from the socket. He thought, "What about all the other lighted bulbs?" but his mother told him to not be a wiseass and to just shut up.

He hated the light tonight, as he carried her body to his car. He loaded her into the back seat and looked around. He felt safe.

He looked again and doubled over in spasms of uncontrollable laughter. He was facing the biggest hole in the ragged fence facing the Air Command. All his fear and caution about being seen was suddenly nonsense for his car was only a few steps from his door. The moon was shining brightly through the largest hole in the fence and Brantley saw a familiar figure advancing toward him—a figure he had feared his whole life. He screamed and jumped into the car slamming the door.

He turned to face the fence and there was nothing there but the moon shining through that jagged hole. He laughed and slammed his hands on the steering wheel. Then he screamed in pain as blood spurted from his cut hand and it began to throb for the first time.

Somehow he started the car and began to ease it across the parking lot. Driving carefully and slowly he guided the Honda out the back pole gate of the La Mancha; it took forever for the pole to go up so he could pass through. He carefully obeyed the 35 mph speed limit down the Blvd. and turned west onto Highway 98. He was glad he wasn't in his Porsche and wouldn't get blood in it. He saw a patrol car in Fort Walton Beach and was momentarily scared but the car turned off in front of him.

He turned in at the produce stand. By this time his mind was working in what he thought were the logical thoughts of a pilot. He suddenly realized she could be identified by her prints. "You should have brought the sword, Brantley. Now, you'll have to use the machete, Brantley."

He stopped the car, looked up and saw the machete that Freddy had hung over the window of the stand. Freddy always told tourist he cut bananas with it as he laughed.

Brantley slipped out, looked around, and took the machete down. He drove on down the lane and stopped beside Ryan's plane.

He knew Ryan had gone to see his mother, and wouldn't be back until tomorrow. He pulled the body to the edge of the Sound, pulled the sack from her head, and saw that the blood had congealed. He quickly laid one arm on a large rock and hacked and hacked at it until it fell to the ground. The second arm didn't take as long as he laughed, 'I've done this before.' He scooped them up in two of the sacks. He carefully put a Piggly-Wiggle bag over each wrist that he tied with his mother's fancy ribbon.

"Push the rock into the Sound, Brantley. Be neat!"

Almost twenty minutes later he had managed to get the limp body into the empty seat of the plane. He started the little open cockpit Waco and gunned it down the runway. When the plane was well out over the Gulf where he doubted anyone would see him for the sky was filled with dark storm clouds, he worked frantically to get her out of the quilt. He had left enough of the quilt hang into his seat that he hoped to pull it away from the body as he tipped the plane so it would fall out.

He tried and tried, but his mother was not there to help him. The little plane was bobbing and weaving as he bumped around. One the third attempt the body bumped into the overhead wing and nearly caught on the strut of the wing but was half way out of the plane. She couldn't have weighed over a hundred and fifteen pounds, but Brantley couldn't control how she kept falling to the right or left in a weird angle. Terrified he might lose control of the plane that he seldom piloted; he decided to do a roll. As the plane turned up-side-down, it sputtered and nearly coughed to a stop as she went sliding out and falling down through the air. The quilt went sailing through the air after her. He frantically completed the roll, gunned the engine and roared away.

Brantley didn't realize it, but he had flown directly in front of the beach at the La Mancha.

He found some bleach in Ryan's washroom and scrubbed the seat of the plane. He had a can of fuel in the Honda which he always carried for his own plane, and he poured enough of it in the tank to make up for what he used. He felt good about how he had done things.

He loaded the two Piggly Wiggly sacks into the trunk, drove up to the produce stand, hung the machete back over the window and headed back to Destin to get the Porsche and go home. He hoped the blood wouldn't leak from the PW bags in his trunk.

He would be flying away to some rig in the morning. The bags and her clothes would be going with him.

His mother had not told him to clean-up the machete.

27

Brantley at the Rig

He landed the Sikorsky S-333 as smooth as sitting down in a chair. The big rotors wound down to a stop as he exited his cabin and opened the door for the three company officials to disembark. He loved the Sikorsky; it was fast—up to about 200 mph, could fly 320 miles on one load of fuel, and it was easy to handle. This morning's trip was only marred for him because one of the men had to sit beside him in the other cockpit seat.

He had made it to Mobile with time to spare, and had time to check the copter and stashed his gear and the bag. He loaded all the equipment they were taking with them telling one of them he didn't need help for he had his own system of loading the copter.

The three company men stood on the copter pad looking out over long stretches of the Gulf seeing another rig way off in the distance; Brantley thought they would never get off the pad. When they had disappeared down the ladder to the level below, he left the copter too, and walked over to the ladder, peered down to see if all was clear, and then descended to the level below the copter pad.

He shook hands with a fellow he knew from Mary Ester, asked how long he had been away from home and said not much was happening there or in Fort Walton next door. The man was called to do some job and Brantley was left alone.

He looked around making certain no one was around, and then he took the duffle bag and threw it way out and saw it sink into the Gulf. No one would ever find the bag with the Nihongo and the two hands in it.

He was really sorry for that had been his favorite of the swords his uncle had left him but he had thought it must disappear also. Brantley took a deep breath, swayed a little, and started laughing. He had done it. He had gotten away with murder.

He laughed for a long time, but it gradually turned into crying— crying just like the boy who wet his pants in grade school because he was ashamed to go to the restroom, like the same high school kid who was afraid to take a shower after football practice. They would laugh at him... She had laughed at him... And then Brantley leaned over the rail clutching his stomach against the hard metal.

At that moment, Brantley wanted his mom so bad! He caught himself mumbling "Mommy! Mommy!" so loudly he feared someone would hear and he clamped his hand over his mouth, but there was a wind today and no one had heard. Brantley knew he would never be punished by his mother again. He had taken care of that. Now, when he became that helpless little boy that he could not wipe out of his mind, he had no one to run to.

He regained his composure and became the helicopter pilot again, straightened his uniform, walked over to the steps leading back up to the copter pad, and leaned on the rail. He waited for what seemed a long time to him until the three company men returned satisfied with what they had seen on the rig, mounted the steps, and opened the passenger doors for them. Once again, he was in charge as he flew them to another rig to inspect. He felt with pride that he could take care of any situation now.

He wondered what was happening back at the La Mancha. He jumped a little as he pictured that other terrified face.

28

Trouble in the Water

Like many young men of his age, Paul has become an avid lover of the Gulf. I wouldn't call him a 'beach bum,' but he could be if he weren't such a responsible young man.

His favorite activity is paddle boarding. I have seen him go down with his long board and the paddle on hundreds of late afternoons, push his board into the water, step on the board with a fluid motion, and dip the paddle is just enough to surf across the waves headed for the shore. He is good at it, better than most, and it appears to be his place where he can go and be alone. I often see his silhouette as he is outlined in the sitting sun; a new Huck Finn standing tall and straight on his raft making decisions about his future.

Because of the commotion going on at the La Mancha, Trish let Paul go to Orlando and, of course, he had invited Doogs to go with him. Paul thought about asking his mom if Roche could go, but he knew she wouldn't approve; he hated being away from Roche. He was glad when Roche told him she and her family were going to Maine for two weeks to visit her mom's aunt. They told each other goodbye several times, and he texted her almost every day he was gone.

Trish drove them to Pensacola because Paul refused to fly from Valparaiso. The boys were eager to see The Mouse, and explore the beach west of Orlando. They spent three days at the Happiest Place in the World, and then drove over to the beach at Clearwater where Trish's cousin has a place near the water. Paul was eager to get on a paddle board and lose himself in yet another body of water he could explore. Doogs just wanted to lie on the sand and get a tan to cover his freckles. He knew it never worked, but he tried.

We don't get many sharks in the Gulf, almost none up in our area of the Panhandle, but they seem to be coming into the Gulf more and more down along the southern coasts of the state.

As Paul went out to make his first run parallel to the line of waves rushing toward the shore, a Great White entered the bay about a quarter of a mile away. She hadn't eaten since yesterday and she smelled fish and another smell she had no concern about. She glided quickly through the water circling in bigger and bigger circles. She was in thirty feet of water and close to the bottom when she saw the shape of a large fish off toward a line of waves headed toward the beach. Instinct told her it was big and she would have to hit it hard to knock it into the air so she could catch it coming down. But now it was gone and she was confused as she darted back and forth trying to locate her prey.

And then it was there again coming slowly back into the water from the shore, but it quickly turned and was swimming parallel to the shore in a big wave. In a flash she was in the wave. She shot to the surface and clamped down on the end of Paul's board. His left foot was near the end and she took half of it as she submerged. Paul felt the sharp pain and the sting of the salty water on his foot and saw the water turning a bloody copper as the wave catapulted him into shallow water.

Doogs had seen what happened from the shore, and in spite of his terror, his bravery saved Paul's life. He splashed out into the waist deep water hollering for Paul to hang on and crying at the same time. He swam into the bloody water fearing the shark might return and hoisted Paul on his back and carried him to shore.

Paul was losing a lot of blood and Doogs knew to tie his towel tightly at Paul's ankle to try to hold the flow of blood. People came running from every direction. An ambulance sped down the boardwalk in a few minutes and Paul was rushed to a little hospital nearby. He was in shock and critical condition because of all the blood he had lost.

Doogs didn't sleep that night. It would not be the last time he cried all night.

29
Marvin Discovers the Evidence

Trish flew down to Orlando and drove over to the hospital where Paul was now recuperating. He left foot was bandaged heavily and he realized he probably wouldn't be playing football anymore. Doogs had sat in the waiting room during Paul's operation, and now slept on a bed next to him. He was a true friend, Paul knew.

I was thankful she had all those many air miles, and knew she would need many more to get them all home. Since I had known her, I hadn't appreciated until now what the woman was accomplishing all by herself. Then, I remembered a little lady who took care of me and my siblings long ago when she was the only one that was left for us. It's remarkable what a strong woman can do.

I agreed to take care of Paul's aquarium while they were gone. His room was not in very good order—typical, for a teenage boy, I thought. I was cleaning their condo when I heard someone at the door. Marvin said he had heard of the horrible accident and was wondering if he could do anything. He saw I was trying to get the place in order, so he pitched in to help. We talked about the body from the Gulf and what Morat seemed to be doing or not doing.

Marvin smiled and said, "Morat is doing just what I think he should be doing."

I looked at him but he turned and starting picking up a pile of clothes on the floor and walked into the bathroom to put them in the hamper.

When he came back I asked, "What do you mean he's doing just what you think he should be?"

"He's keeping everyone on their toes and wondering just how much he knows, and that way someone will make a mistake if that person is still around. Now, I'm not saying he knows he's doing that, but he is."

I started to ask what he meant by 'if that person is still around,' but as he picked up Paul's car washing equipment, the zip bag of crack fell out of the bucket on to the floor.

Marvin knew instantly what was in the bag, and I did too for I have seen other teenagers in trouble. We both stood for a moment looking at each other.

I immediately said, "I don't believe it. I know Paul. I'm not so close I've lost my sense. He never would have anything to do with this. He's top in his class and a star athlete, but he's a decent man too. I don't believe this at all! He's been to my condo many times studying and writing. I've had a little experience with teenagers and Paul is not a user."

"Hey, calm down Prof. I really don't believe it's his either," Marvin said. "But why is it in his bucket? This is really trouble for him, and you know we have to turn it over to the police. I've had experience also, and I don't think he is a user either, but what about if he's getting it somewhere and selling? You know how concerned he is with helping his mother, saving her money she would have spent on him, and watching the bills. He's still a teenager, and sometimes, as you know, they don't think things through. But you do know the police have to be notified."

I shuddered when I thought of Morat, and blurted out, "Not to Okaloosa County. To the State...to J C Blevins."

Marvin agreed and we contacted J C who arrived about an hour later. J C remembered he was the one who question Trish and Paul down in the gazebo according to Morat's directions, and he didn't believe Paul used cocaine either.

Both of them were concerned if for some stupid reason Paul was selling to his classmates, but none of us believed it.

"It obviously was put into the bucket, but just like a teenager his attention got diverted, on his girlfriend on the beach—or something else, and he just forgot all about it and took off," I insisted.

J C nodded and said, "That's one answer," and Marvin agreed, but we were all concerned and puzzled.

We waited, and when Trish and Paul arrived back home four weeks later on July 16th, I waited until I thought they were settled in. Paul still spent a lot of time in bed, and after the long flight home, I imagined that was where he would be. I knocked on the door and Trish greeted me with a hug and kiss on the cheek. I looked at her and saw how tired and strained she looked. She appeared ten years older than when I had seen her last. I asked if I could see Paul, and she said he didn't want to see me. I was surprised until she explained he didn't want me to see him down like he was. I promised to try to put him at ease, and she looked appreciative.

He was lying in bed with his left leg elevated on a big pillow. He started to object to me being there, but turned his head and I could see the beginning of tears. I walked over the bed and reached out and messed up his hair. He flinched and really started to cry. He kept saying that he had caused his mother so much trouble and that he could never repay her. I hushed him and said she loved him more than herself and he was the only man she had. That was not the right thing to say, but I didn't know it.

The tears, which surely had been pent-up for days while he was in the hospital, really started.

I finally broke the tension by telling him he owed me good money for cleaning his room. I laughed as I said he ought to keep his car cleaning business outside in the storage unit. He looked startled, and I realized he knew what we had found.

"You found the stuff, didn't you?"

"Marvin did. Where did you get it?"

He looked straight at me and told me where he had found it under the front seat of Chuck Jenkins's Cadillac. He said that Saturday he was finishing the car when he felt it under the front driver's seat and then Roche had called him and he just forgot about the bag.

I believed him.

So did Marvin, and so did J C Blevins, for at that moment J C knocked on the door and Marvin was with him.

They questioned him for almost half an hour, it seemed, but they believed him. They knew Paul's reputation in the community, but they also knew Chuck had not been in any trouble. They also knew it would just be Paul's word against Chuck's.

Later that night, I realized my suspicions about Marvin all this time were wrong. He was too knowledgeable about what was going on and J C seemed trust him and discuss events with him.

I didn't know it then, but that was the big break the State Police needed for finding out how so much drugs were coming in to the Panhandle. Blevins had sure been tight lipped as I hadn't even realized he knew Marvin. That's when Marvin started watching the Gulf every night, late into the night, but I didn't know that either.

30
Escape

Brantley knew he was in trouble; he heard on his headphones that he was a suspect. None of the company officials with him seemed to know anything about it, and when he flew them back to Mobile, he touched down, got them out, and took off again. They were surprised and looked really dumbfounded as two State Patrol cars raced toward the Sikorsky where he had landed. He banked the copter back toward the Gulf, saw one of the patrolmen out by his car and could see that he was on his phone.

Brantley knew exactly what he was going to do. There are over 1700 oil rigs in the Gulf around Mobile Bay, and he knew all the rigs belonging to his company. His chart showed their exact location and he knew the company chart in the office at Mobile did too, but he knew the ones that didn't have anyone on them because he was the only one who flew personal out to them. He thought he could go from one to another for several weeks and not be caught. He had supervised which rigs had extra fuel for the Sikorsky. Brantley was pleased.

His finger throbbed with pain and looked infected, but there wasn't a first-aid kit on the Sikorsky for some reason.

He flew to one of the rigs and threw tarps over the copter and felt safe for some time. Then he moved from empty rig to empty rig during the nights and was hidden for days while he figured out what his final plan would be. He was in his element, he was in charge. He had deactivated the location transmitter on the Sikorsky. He was the only pilot, and how would anyone be able to pinpoint his company's empty rigs from the shore and be able to fly to them, he reasoned. He felt safe.

And now three weeks later, he was landing on yet another rig he knew was unmanned. He found a snack machine that still had several items left in it. He knew the candy bars and bags of chips would probably be stale, however he took a long bar and smashed at the machine, taking several minutes to smash through the Plexiglas. Stabs of pain shot through his hand as he smashed at the machine, but he now had food to last at least another week.

He tore into a candy bar and found that though it had turned that white color like they do when they get hot, it was still delicious. He counted his stash of them—thirteen. Along with the candy, he had an assortment of snacks but noticed that many of them contained much salt and he had little water. Now, he thought, find something to drink.

Brantley was feeling good about himself. He was in charge and didn't need anyone to make decisions for him. His hand hurt and was swollen, in fact, it was throbbing.

31
Two of a Kind

Josephine tried to speak with Chuck Jenkins since she had come to the Island. She knew where he lived and that he took the Lollipop out into the Gulf on a regular basis. She also knew what was happening when he took the bright blue and white yacht out for she had her binoculars and she watched. She finally waited for him one day when he was at lunch at Tides Inn and encountered him as he came out.

Chuck turned away from her in disgust as he saw her, but she caught up to him and said in a hoarse, nervous almost whisper, "Chuck, I need to talk with you."

"I have nothing to say to you."

"But I know what you are doing, and if I can find out so easily, others can too."

Chuck hesitated and looked around nervously and snarled at her, "I'll pick you up at the La Mancha tonight about midnight."

"No, I'll meet you at the boat in Pensacola."

He thought he should have been surprised she knew where the boat was, but he wasn't, "Okay, but be on time."

She drove the forty miles thinking what she would say to Chuck. She parked her car in a line of cars near the boat slip, and was walking down the pier when *Lollipop's* engines roared awake.

"Hurry up, and get aboard, Damn it, before anyone sees you."

She stumbled getting on the loading platform of the big boat and climbed the three steps up to the back deck. She hadn't been in a boat for years and she was wobbly. Chuck backed the yacht out, spun it around almost knocking her over, and they were headed for the open waters of the Gulf.

The boat seemed to know where it was going, or Chuck was so angry and distracted, for soon they saw the lights of the La Mancha shining from the shore about a mile away.

"What do you want from me," Chuck growled.

"I just want to talk, and to let you know I know about the drugs you pick up out here. They're wrapped in heavy sheets of plastic and then burlap so they are inconspicuous in the water. I've seen you several times."

Chuck jumped up from the little table where they had sat down and slammed his fist on the railing and Josephine thought he might attack her.

She said, "And I want to tell you that I love you, always have, and will till I die."

"Shut up! Just shut up! Why did you have to go away and come back into my life as the grotesque thing that you are? You were my best friend...the one I turned to when Launie was on my case...the one I looked up to for advice... Why? Damn it to Hell, Why?"

"I did it because Launie always treated those girls better than she did us. It got to where she didn't have the time of day for me, but when I came back from Europe, she wouldn't talk to me...just like you..."

"But, you were my big brother. You were Joe. You were my hero... the one I told everything too. God, I loved you more than anything because we just had each other. She was our mom, or yeah, but she wasn't the one we went home to because she was never there. I hated her, and I hated her more after you came back.

But, I hated you more! Why? Why, I asked. What a screwed-up mess we have all made. A mother who wouldn't tell us who our dad is, or was... A mother who ran her business and never had a home for us. You and I living in that mess. Fixing our own food, sharing everything... You, the only one I had— and you did THAT to yourself. I hate you and my whole insane life."

"Chuck, I'm so sorry. I thought she would notice me this way. I thought if I looked like her and talked like her as a woman, she would take me into her life. All I got though was her year old Caddy and the envelope of money she sends by one of the girls twice a month. And your scorn... Chuck, please look at me... Please forgive me. Please?"

Josephine stood and started toward him, but he backed away in disgust. She stopped, unsure of her footing, and stumbled.

In their hurry to leave Pensacola, one of the gates from the loading pad had not been fastened securely.

When she stumbled, she fell and hit her head on the sharp corner of the table ripping a big gash in her forehead.

She passed out, hit the unlatched gate, and tumbled off the back of the yacht. She hit the water and went under for the first time.

Chuck scrambled to the platform where she had been as she came up the second time. He jumped off, dove under the water and tried to find her in the dark water, but the water of the Gulf tonight was as black as the Sound always is. As he came to the surface, she was nowhere to be seen.

He dove again and again and swam in every direction so many times he couldn't swim anymore. He didn't realize that she was stuck under the boat. The big Marlineer 44 had a thick keel running down the middle of the bottom and she was lodged up against it.

He hadn't realized either how long they had been out there, but as he struggled to climb back aboard, the sun blinded his tear-filled eyes as it came up on the horizon. He sat with his legs dangling from the back loading ramp and cried. He was there several minutes as all the hurt and rage he had felt for over five years poured out of him.

Finally, it was all gone, he started the yacht, didn't see her body dislodge behind the boat, and he guided the boat slowly away from the spot he would mark in his mind forever. He had tried to find her; but, he didn't.

How would he live with this? A few hours ago, his life was anger and disgust at himself for doing the things he did, but now it was worse. How would he tell Launie? What would he say? Then he thought she probably won't give a damn anyway. He straightened the *Lollipop* as he realized it was just drifting and headed toward the pass at Destin so he could come back down the bay and tie up near the Dorm.

He would have to tell her Joe was dead somewhere out there in the water.

32

Launie's Little Box

Launie backhanded Chuck so hard he fell against the little table that held her liquor. He and the table crashed to the floor and he felt liquid running down his right arm. Launie was crazed and she kicked him square in the stomach and then gashed his forehead and scalp with her long painted false nails. Chuck grabbed her foot and tripped her onto the floor where they sat and slapped each other for several minutes. The first slaps were vicious, but gradually they weakened and the two of them fell into each other's arms. Chuck couldn't remember when his mother had hugged him, much less cried into his shoulder.

But Launie was quickly the old Launie again, and she hissed, "You have to go back out there and find her. You can't let her stay out there. A shipment will be dumped in a couple of days and we can't have her found and police boats snooping around."

Chuck hated her with all his being as she said that. Joe was dead out there in the water, and all she cared about was maybe getting her load of stuff intercepted. That's exactly what he had thought on his way back on the *Lollipop*. He hit her as hard as he could; as she went tumbling against the patio doors, he took the little box off the table by her bed and stuffed it into his shirt.

"I'll go try to find him, but not for you, you're nothing. You caused all this because of your greed. We meant nothing to you. You're crazy… you're nothing…but you are evil. I'll find him and take him away and never see you lying filthy face again. I hope you burn in Hell."

He knew he better leave before he hurt her bad. He was ready to kill her, but he was not like his mother. As he started out the door, he saw the box Launie was fixing to send to Miami.

He tore open the lid and found it as he thought he would, full of neatly stacked large denomination bills. He picked it up and went out the door.

She hadn't said a word. She knew she had many more in the safe behind that padded headboard of her big purple bed.

He ran out of the crazy house where Launie lived with her girls, down the pier and powered up the Lollipop. Maybe, he thought, this will be the last time I pilot this beautiful thing.

He pushed the throttle open as he whizzed down the Sound between the Island and the mainland headed toward Pensacola. Businesses were opening for the day along the waterfront in Fort Walton Beach. Traffic was tied up at the light just before Brooks Bridge crossed the Sound.

He slowed the *Lollipop* as he neared the new construction on the Fort Walton Beach side of the Sound just a few hundred yards west of the La Mancha complex on the other side. Okaloosa County was building a new jail on the bank of the Sound with a dock for the water patrol boats underneath. Chuck knew he had to mind all the rules as he went by it each trip he made down the Sound.

He maneuvered the yacht through the barge channel around the little island someone had name "Egg." Then he was glad to have the open water to himself again as he was safely past. There was a large barge coming up from the West, but there was plenty of room for both of them.

His forehead stung from the scratches, but he knew it would be the last time she would hurt him. Tears continued to fill his eyes and run down his cheeks which he couldn't control and didn't even try to.

About forty-five minutes later he pulled the yacht into the slip at Pensacola and saw Joe's car parked over in a parking lot. He knew the keys would be in it for they always were. He got in and sat for a few minutes. Then, he started the car and headed north for Interstate 10. He would just keep driving. He smelled the scent of Josephine in the car and the car screeched onto the shoulder of the street as his foot slammed on the brake. He sat for a long time and hurt in his chest began to come again. He had no idea how long he was there, but he turned the car back toward the pier, parked it, got out and went to the boat. He also had no idea how he was going to do it, but he had to find Joe. He had to.

The big boat was powered by two diesel engines with a total of over a thousand horse power and as he pushed the throttle open, it roared over the water until a few minutes later it was in front of the La Mancha. For an hour he guided the boat crisscrossing the water several times. His heart was breaking, but he also knew Joe was dead. Then, he realized the futility of it and whipped the boat around and headed back to Pensacola.

He got into the Caddy, was at Interstate 10 in thirty minutes, and headed toward Atlanta. He had the clothes on his back, the box full of money and the little black box, a year old Caddy and a peace of mind he hadn't ever had.

He had no regrets about the penthouse for all it had in it were a bed and his personal things; he did think about all his shoes and clothes that had cost so much. The frig was full of nothing but junk food, mostly half-full pizza boxes or Japanese carry out boxes he'd ordered in and forgotten about. He'd miss his gym where he worked out and his bicycle.

He grimaced when he thought of the half empty bottle of Dewar's White Label Scotch he and Joe always liked that he had bought during a weak moment one night when he had wanted to see Joe so bad.

Suddenly he thought of that little dog, Skipper, and wondered what would happen to him.

He would ditch the Caddy somewhere or roll it into a swamp, and no one would ever find him.

33

Chuck Escapes from it All

The car whizzed east on Interstate 10 toward Tallahassee and a plan formulated in Chuck's mind. He pulled into a rest area, shuffled through the glove box of Joe's Caddy and found a map of Florida. Southern Alabama was on the map too, and on the spur of the moment, Chuck decided to go to Dothan, Alabama.

Something caused him to drive west a few miles to Enterprise. As he pulled into the town, he realized the beginning of the Choctawhatchee River was not far away, and he thought what irony it would be to find a secluded place on the river and drive the car into it. Maybe it would drift all the way back to the Bay for that's where the river ended. He smiled at his crazy idea, but decided to do it.

He rented a cheap motel room for two nights. He would leave the next morning before dawn, find the spot on the river to get rid of the car, get back to Enterprise somehow, stay another night, and then take the Grey Hound into Dothan.

It took him several hours to find a high bank above the river that was secluded. He drove down what he thought was a fishing trail but it was not a road at all. The branches of the trees along the path scratched the sides of the car; the tires sunk into deep mud puddles and once into a wide ditch that he thought had stopped his progress. He rocked the car back and forth by putting it into reverse and then into drive as quickly as he could and finally had made it to the other side of the ditch.

At the end of the path was a burned out camp fire, many 'dead soldiers' and more used condoms than he had ever seen, he thought. This was a party place, and Chuck laughed out loud as he thought about some dude peeing off the bank and seeing the submerged Cadillac. He drove to the edge of the high bank, got out and found a large rock, and with the driver's door open, he put the car in drive and slammed the rock on the gas pedal. The big car sailed off the edge of the bank and landed about fifteen feet out in the river. He stood on the bank as the car slowly sank to the bottom. He was surprised to see it sink even further as the bottom was obviously thick mud and debris. By accident, he had selected a spot where even he had a hard time seeing the car as he stood there on the bank.

Chuck turned and started back up the path to the road. Coming down the path was a really big man with a rifle under one arm. For a second, Chuck was shaken but the man smiled, whistled for his dog which appeared from the bushes, and greeted Chuck with, "Seen any rabbits, down here?" Chuck smiled back and said that he had heard of this place and his curiosity had caused him to walk the three-fourths of a mile to see what was down there. As he went on up to the road, he was happy that the man hadn't asked about where was his car?

When he got up to the road he started walking down toward Enterprise; within a quarter of a mile an old farmer stopped in his pick-up and offered him a ride into town. The man raised pigs and Chuck was happy when they had reached town. He walked to the little motel where he had his room, took a shower, checked the disappearing scab where Launie had gashed his forehead, and went to Whataburger for supper. He was in bed by nine so he could get up at six and catch the Grey Hound to Dothan.

Dothan was large enough that Chuck figured he wouldn't attract too much attention. No one would know who he was, and besides, he wasn't in any kind of trouble. He checked in at Holiday Inn Express and paid for three days. He had no intention of staying for three nights, but no one would be bothering him before the day he was to check-out.

He had seen the Bells Department store on the way into town, and since it wasn't a long walk, he was there in five minutes. Searching through

117

the luggage department, Chuck found eight rolling tote bags. They were large enough he hoped as he paid for them.

On the way back to the motel, he stopped at Supershears where the Asian lady was very surprised when he said he wanted a color job.

"Why do you want to ruin that lovely black hair?"

"I've been through a bad divorce and I just thought it might be a start over if I change my appearance too. I want you to bleach it really light. I guess I want to be a blonde!

They have more fun, you know?"

She laughed and said, "Yeah, I guess! Sure, I will do it for you. I suppose you want your eye brows bleached too? Where did you get that painful looking wound on your head?"

"Where would you think, I got it? Yes, I don't want any of my ex-wife's friends to recognize me the next time I bump into them."

Forty-five minutes later Chuck looked at himself in her mirror and nearly didn't recognize himself. He laughed, paid and tipped her a twenty.

He found the eight tote bags waiting for him at the desk, delivered to his motel just as the lady at Bells had promised; of course, he had paid the taxi that delivered them. When he had them in his room, the first thing he checked was the wall safe making sure his box of money was safe.

The next morning he was at Bells by the time it opened where he bought four leisure outfits which he thought looked sharp and expensive. They certainly weren't what he was used to wearing but he did find two Polo tops.

This time he took a taxi to the motel, had it wait for him while he showered and put on the best looking suit. He said he wanted to go to the Buick dealership and soon he was looking at new cars.

He decided on a cherry red 2014 Lacrosse with just about everything on it imaginable. When he counted out $33, 695, the manager of the dealership looked surprised--maybe suspicious, but Chuck explained a recent stinky divorce where she had the car, and he had decided to get what money from his bank account that he could. Money talks and the manager wrote out a promise of oil changes and waxing for a year. Chuck smiled.

As he drove away from the motel where he had picked up his things, he started looking at the fields and groves of trees as he past them. He had never noticed nature before, not even the Gulf where he had lived all his life, first in New Orleans which he didn't remember much about, and then in Fort Walton Beach.

He realized that his life didn't amount to much and that Launie had always controlled it. He wondered what other kids had done, what games they had played, what movies they went to see, that he didn't because Joe and he had only had each other. He had been home schooled by a fat old man who smelled bad, and he wondered what he and Joe hadn't learned that high school kids learned together at school. He had never had a girlfriend and knew nothing about women; oh, he wasn't gay he knew because he had had enough girls, but he didn't know anything about them.

He headed for Fort Walton Beach with a new plan for a new life.

34
The Crows this Morning

We also have crows at the La Mancha; big ones that compete with the gulls for whatever they find to eat. They're out in force this morning cawing in harsh calls from the roofs of both the Pelican and the Dolphin that face the Gulf while three are hopping and skidding back and for on the metal roof of the gazebo right in front of the water, shrieking I guess about their territory being invaded.

I've been to London several times and have seen the ravens that are supposed to be guarding The Tower of London, but these crows are bigger and have what look like just as heavy sharp beaks. They also don't have their wings clipped like the ravens do. They fly in groups it seems and I have seen gulls divert their flight to get out of the way of the crows. And, of course, in my opinion they are hundreds of times smarter than the gulls.

I see Bicycle Bob as he is riding down the walk from the parking lot in front of the Pelican which runs parallel to the big pool next to the beach. He continues on up the slope of the boardwalk into the gazebo. He pauses on the bike, scans the Gulf, makes a circle in the gazebo, comes back down the slope and turns right at the end to coast along the walk which goes along the end of my building.

The crows are annoyed and one takes a dive at Bob as he goes along the walk. The crow whacks Bob on the head and I see a spot of red that is spreading. Bob pumps harder and looks over his shoulder with amazement; I know he won't admit it, but with a little fear too.

I have never seen the crows, or any other bird show that kind of aggression around here, or anywhere else for that matter.

Then for some reason they all fly up into the air—all of them from all the rooftops—two dozen or more, form into a bunch and they all fly far out over the water. They never do that as they seem to have an aversion to being over a big stretch of water. They just never do that and yet they are so far out that they are just tiny black specks to me.

As they head back into shore flying faster now, they scatter into a frenzy of flapping wings but they swirl up into another bunch squawking and hitting each other with their wings and pecking frantically. They all coast in and land on the low white rock wall right in front of where Jonathan L is sitting on the volleyball goal post—he immediately flies away. That section is also right down in front of my balcony; they line up almost in a row all looking out at the Gulf.

Crows just don't do what they are doing; they never sit in a row or get that close to the ground unless they are eating something. They seem to be waiting for something and they are not very patient. They move around restlessly taking pecks at one another. I realize there is nothing playful going on as a fight ensues with three attacking one on top of the flat capstone of one of the fence columns. There's something savage about their attack as they flutter into the air pecking at one of their own. It falls over the edge of the wall into the lawn, struggles to get up, staggers away in a limping run, and manages to get into the air and lands on top of the gazebo while its caws fill the air like screams.

I have never seen this behavior before; it is ominous and I feel a twinge of dread. I look around to see if anyone is watching, and get what I know is a sheepish grin on my face. I don't think of Peter Seller's funny remark about 'swine birds,' but Hitchcock comes to mind.

35

Oh No, Not Again

Brantley is still free in the Gulf somewhere he only knows about. This morning the beach is filled already with people from all over the South—new visitors who haven't heard about the body on our beach. The license plates on the cars at the La Mancha always include most of the Southern states and dozens more from north the Mason-Dixon Line. Max has the beach lined with the big blue umbrellas and the beach chairs standing in symmetrical rows for which he is so proud. Dozens of bodies of all shapes and sizes are sizzling in the sun trying for that perfect tan.

The beach sun flower vines almost surround the gazebo with a dazzle of bright yellow blossoms. How it got its name is a mystery to me for the flowers look almost like daisies, not sunflowers, but they are bright yellow. They are healthy and full of blooms because the water from the showers where people wash off the sand from the beach runs down into them.

Sometimes I think my thoughts would be weird to others. Last night I sat on my balcony looking out at the Gulf and the strangest idea came to me.

Is there a place out there in the Gulf where a free floating object would stand still? A sort of dead place in the water where nothing moves in any direction? What would cause it to finally be pulled in one direction? A breeze? The wake of a passing boat? Some other object already moving in one direction bumping into it?

Little did I know that as I took my coffee out on the balcony this morning that an object was on its way to our beach moving slowly but steadily through the currents to finally be picked up by the waves and pushed or slammed into our beach. But it was on its way, and no one knew it and nothing would stop it.

All those people on the beach coated with lotion, all the kids running in the shallows screaming with laughter, all those dozing in the beach chairs had no idea what was going to totally ruin their day.

I was cleaning my little electric grill that I had used a couple of nights ago. Electric ones were all we are allowed on our balconies, and I miss the smell and taste of charcoal when I cook something on it.

Then I heard the noise start.... It was a dog barking and I finally realized that it was Skipper, Josephine's little back, tan, and white Corgi. Skipper was consistent with his barking which turned to a high howling and sounded like he was hurt. He howled way too long before I finally went down the elevator, crossed over to the Dolphin, took the elevator up to the sixth floor, and walked down to 62 where Skipper was sitting now growling fiercely at the front door. He had jumped out an open kitchen window it appeared, and now couldn't get back into the condo.

There are very few people that Skipper would come to except Josephine, but he turned to me and whimpered. I picked him up and started knocking on the door. But Skipper would never walk with Josephine again for what was left of her was about to wash up on our beach.

One of the paddle boarders out about five hundred yards saw it first. It looked alive he would tell Morat later. He had fallen off his board, managed to jump back on, and hurriedly rode the next waves into shore. Then some kids out trying to ride waves on their boogie boards saw it and screamed like a shark was in the water. Two little boys were building sandcastles, and as one ran to get some water, he froze. Mylee, who comes every day to fish threw her rod and reel up into the air, and retreated to the shore from the waist deep water she was in.

It hit the sandbar about a hundred feet out, paused, and was washed over it with the next wave. Gulls filled the air swirling and diving and shrieking but they were no match for the crows already there.

There was chaos on the beach as people ran to where it could be seen from the shore.

The crows had covered the bobbing mass and were cawing, jumping up in little leaps only as crows do spraying blood from their flapping wings, and then diving back down where dozens of others were pecking away madly. Some blue crabs had attached to it, and a dead jelly fish was on one thigh.

Max stood like a stone. Terror filled his eyes and his vomit spurted out and ran down his own chest. He couldn't move, it appeared, and then he ran faster than I had ever seen him, much faster than the time before, yelling for someone to call Morat.

The horrible mass nudged up to our beach just a few yards from where the first body had landed.

36

Respect

The devilish side of me wanted to laugh as I thought about what Morat would look like when he realized there was another body. He probably would have something like an epileptic seizure. But, it really wasn't funny, and I knew my laugh was just a nervous cover-up of the dread what would happen the rest of the day and next few weeks.

Morat arrived. He looked very strained and like he hadn't slept much. He looked so much older than a few weeks ago when I first met him. At least we all knew who this had been by the big blue Safire ring on her finger and her familiar clothes. The coroner said she had been in the water for some time and that was apparent. The body was bloated and had that ghastly blue color that cadavers get. Her clothes were gather tightly in the wrong places and she looked vulgar—I wanted her covered but Morat insisted we investigate first. The coroner found the big gash on her head through all the mess the water and the crows had done to her and concluded we had another possible murder on our hands.

Morat's problem was that no one knew who Josephine Jones really was. No one knew where she came from. She had paid cash for her condo so there were no mortgage agreements. The Cadillac was missing. It might be a clue, but it might take days to find it.

When Marvin had opened her condo for Morat, they found it was furnished with tasteful beach type furniture and that everything was neat and in order. They found Skipper's bowl on the floor of the kitchen with his bag of food on the counter above. A change of outfits lay on her bed like she had just changed to something else and left to go somewhere. The condo was bare of any personal things—extremely bare, like she had no past, or didn't want to remember a past. Morat was no closer to knowing anything of her death than he was with the first one.

However, they also found stacks and stacks of $50 bills.

Morat wasn't popping chocolate kisses today. He was eating Tums.

When Doc Wells did the autopsy in the morgue of the new jail, he saw those other scars on the body, the operation scars that so disgusted Chuck, but he never said anything to anyone about them until over a year later.

37

Anger on the Balcony

At first he had been apprehensive of going to the La Mancha, but he thought the only ones there who had known him was Paul and the retired school teacher. He looked in the visor mirror and hardly recognized himself, so he decided to go for it. He had several fake identification cards which he had carried for years as Launie was always afraid he would expose her if he were caught. One of them was taken when he had been in the sun all summer, and his hair was sort of bleached out. It would have to do.

He rented the condo insisting on the Dolphin building saying a friend said it had the best views of the Gulf. Cathy in the rental office had told him the Pelican had just as good a view and that there was a really nice one on the sixth floor. But Chuck got his way, and it was next door to Joe's old place. He had never been to the La Mancha, but was pleased with the condo and especially with the view.

But that morning he had watched in horror as the kid on the beach and all the other people had watched Joe's body wash up on the beach. He was so ashamed for Joe that they had seen him that way. He wanted so much to hurry down and help.

He was shaving when he heard the first commotion, and as he stood watching standing back from the railing of his balcony, he touched his chin and saw blood on his fingers as he looked at his hand. Chuck had been taught to be tough and that boys don't cry, but tears welled up in his eyes as they had so many times recently, and he saw in his mind the blood running down Joe's face when he had slipped and fallen onto the corner of the table on the Lollipop, and now he cried as he had on the way back to Pensacola. Chuck surprised himself as he realized he was sobbing uncontrollably remembering how he could not find Joe and had given up his search.

His anguish turned to anger as he watched for what seemed hours as some silly looking little man dressed in white pants had held up getting Joe's body off the beach and away from all those stares.

He watched as the medics lifted Joe's body into the body bag and onto the gurney and as they struggled to get him up the ramp to the gazebo and then into the ambulance sitting on the lawn below him. He wanted to follow the ambulance but realized he would call attention to himself, so he waited.

During the night, a downpour erased all signs of the day before from the beach. The local weatherman reported that the Panhandle had received more rain this July than in the last fifty Julys.

The next morning Chuck went to the lobby and bought a copy of the NorthWest Daily from the machine. It was the front page story, of course, and he found out that it was the second body which had washed up on the beach at the La Mancha this summer. He wondered who the first one had been. Then he read the story;

A second body has washed into the beach of the La Mancha this summer. This body was covered with crows as it washed ashore, but the coroner reports that death was caused by a blow to the head. Detective Emile Morat knows who this body was as does everyone at the La Mancha because of the large Safire and diamond ring on her right hand. Josephine Jones who moved into her condo soon after Katrina slammed into New Orleans was a familiar figure around the condo complex. No one is really sure if that was her real name and Morat reports there was no identification found in her condo. She will be interred at Memorial Cemetery this coming Friday at 11.

Chuck wanted a drink so bad, but went in and took a long shower.

38

At Rest Finally

We buried her in Fort Walton Memorial Cemetery. Her headstone simply reads "Josephine Jones" – 2014.

On that Friday, in a heavy rain, we followed the hearse to the cemetery. During a lull in the rain, the minister from the Methodist church said a few words and the cemetery men lower the casket into the ground.

The burial was quick as the rain really started pouring down as it had for the last couple of weeks.

There were only five of us at the cemetery: Morat and his wife Libby, Trooper Blevins, Marvin and me. None of us noticed a young man sitting over on a bench under one of the trees, and wouldn't have thought anything about him if we had, except we might have wondered why anyone would be sitting there in the heavy rain.

We spent some of the money found in her condo on the casket and flowers that Libby had insisted on, and on the headstone of her grave.

About two weeks later the old man who keeps the cemetery lawns saw a good-looking blonde-headed man bring a large bunch of red roses and a very big bottle of Dewar's White Label Scotch to the grave. He said the man knelt by the grave and stayed that way for several minutes.

He said the Scotch was pretty good also…

39

Happy Birthday to Me!

Paul hadn't been down to the water since he arrived home but finally agreed to go so Marvin picked him up in one of the golf carts he uses taking laundry and materials from building to building around the complex. As they crossed the parking lot going to the gazebo, Paul realized that many people were waiting for him. We had strung garlands of crepe paper all the way on the pool fence, wrapped the railings of the boardwalk with it, and the gazebo looked somewhat like a birthday cake for it was Paul's birthday.

At first Paul didn't want to see the other kids and he asked Marvin to please turn around, but Trish who was walking beside the cart put a stop to that.

The crowd of young people from FWBH and Faith Lutheran in Destin cheered loudly as the golf cart pulled up. Those of us a little older in age were sitting at the tables around the pool. Marvin and I estimated later that over a hundred people were there.

He hadn't seen Roche since he returned home as Trish had told her he just wouldn't or couldn't see her yet. She was there waiting for him, and in front of us all, she leaned over and kissed him on the mouth which brought more cheers and whistles from Doogs and his friends. Within fifteen minutes it seemed he had forgotten about his foot and he was just one of them again.

Trish had brought Paul's beach shorts with her and encouraged him to go into the pool house and put them on so he could get into the water but he refused and wouldn't budge. He did go down on the beach wearing what he had on and his Nike shoes which covered his foot and sat with Roche as the others played in the water or lay on the beach talking about whatever young people talk about.

Late in the afternoon Trish called them back to the pool area as the sun was sitting in a blazing glory on the horizon. After opening many, many presents, most of them silly things provided by Doogs and his buddies which brought even more laughs and joking, we had red velvet cake and vanilla ice cream—dessert before the meal, for as soon as the cake and ice cream were gone and Paul had made a little speech about how great everyone was for thinking of him and how happy he was to be back near 'his' water and his friends, the young people loaded into cars to go to Pandora's Steak House where we adults had reserved the banquet room so they could have a prime rib dinner.

But July 19th isn't just Paul's birthday. As she saw the cars leave the La Mancha back gate, Nellie Tromley in her usual fit of rage, threw an empty bottle off her balcony.

Nellie had heard the noise of the party all afternoon as she said brooding on her balcony. Nellie suffers a thinning of the inner ear canal which causes acute hearing. Perhaps part of her becoming an old grouch was because everyone always seems so loud to her and she had tried to make her world quieter.

She heard two of the kids talking about going to Pandora's and thought of the last time she was there. That had been an occasion!

Before noon Nellie had called Quarters, the liquor store just off the Island on 98 with her usual order; a case of Coke Cola and a case of Bacardi. She hurried to dress because she knew Garrett that handsome young college kid from Alabama would be delivering it.

She had waited to call for her weekly order until after she attempted to bake cupcakes so she would have something to serve him. Her mother had always told her to have treats for the young men who came to visit.

He knew not to knock loudly so when she heard the tap on the door, she lifted the edge of the curtain on the kitchen window and peeked through to make sure it was Garrett. She skipped to the front door and threw it open.

He stepped back a foot or two from the sight that appeared in the doorway. When he recovered, he said, "Miss Tromley, here is your order. Shall I sit it on the kitchen counter for you?"

"Yes! Yes! Do come in Garrett. You can sit it with the other bottles I still have. I have made tiny cupcakes for us today! Please come in!"

He sat the boxes of the floor of the kitchen, cut the cartons open with his box-cutter, and sat the bottles in neat rows beside the many that were already on the counter.

"My! My! That looks so nice! You always take care of me so nice, Garrett!"

She said his name in a low soft Southern drawl while she edged closer to him as they stood in the small kitchen.

He towered over her as she moved even closer, but maneuvered himself toward the open front door as he said, "But I must be going back to work. I left my car running and I havea lot of work left before I can go to the beach."

"But you haven't had your cakes and I will pour us a good drinkie as we have them!"

He shuddered as he smelled her breath, "No, not today, I have to go now. Maybe I can stay and visit next time."

"Okay! That would be nice. Here is your tip! You are such a nice young man, Garrett!"

"Thank you, Miss Tromley, as he looked at the three twenties she handed him. "My mother will be glad to hear that."

And now Nellie sat on her balcony with three empty pint Mason fruit jars; 'dead soldiers,' by her feet. She giggled as she saw them and thought that's what her Daddy had called empty beer bottles when he came back from the War. She remember, too, her Granddaddy Gottlieb sealed his "white lightning" in Mason jars. She knew her Granddaddy had made the best moonshine around and had sold many many dollars' worth. But, Nellie was thinking through the fog of her mind how Garrett never ever stayed to have cakes with her.

All afternoon she sat there brooding about no invitation to the birthday party. She had seen Marvin haul Paul to the pool in the golf cart. Paul was the only decent person who lived at the La Mancha she thought; he always waved up at her and said politely, "Good morning, Miss Tromley." But she didn't give a flying fart for that nasty Marvin who was always treating her like a child and trying to tell her what she could or couldn't do.

She saw the party break-up, took another hearty drink from the half-empty jar on the little table next to her, and smoothed the skirt of her party dress.

The sun was almost down behind Sea Turtle, the building west of her. She always complained she couldn't see the sunset from her balcony and in earlier times she would walk around Sea Turtle so she could see it.

She hadn't done that recently she realized. All she could see were the dark outlines of the palms near her balcony.

She saw Marvin and that very ugly retired teacher coming up her sidewalk in the golf cart. She disliked that wiseass teacher with a vengeance. He dared to correct her once long ago when she had said there was no such thing as raisin pie. He had said his grandmother had made them all through the Depression. What a lie! She never spoke to him again.

She saw them go by as she slouched down in her chair so they wouldn't see her. Now she was happy about the shadows for they really could not see her; she wanted so much to throw a bottle at them.

She bided her time and soon saw her nemesis, the teacher walking back by himself.

As she threw the bottle, she shouted, "Take that! Get your stinking Yankee arse off my sidewalk! You lying carpetbagger."

"Hello, Miss Nellie, I greeted her as I jumped back; I looked up and was totally amazed at the apparition which appeared above me.

"Don't 'Howdy' me, you lying scalawag. Go back up North or wherever you belong and tell your dang lies."

She was almost hidden behind the railing and in the twilight it was easy for me to imagine a tired old Southern Faulkner character glaring from the shadows. Nellie was dressed in some flimsy flowered party dress which could have been popular sixty years ago. She had a little tiara on her straight grey-white hair like little girls wear to parties. Every once and a while, she blew one of the party whistles which zip out from a roll and then snap back. Her bright red lips seemed exaggerated against her pale white skin. Her eyes looked sunk into her forehead they were so shadowed.

Climbing up on the chair she always hides in behind her balcony railing, she was singing some eerie song. I watch in amazement as she stepped up and put one foot on the top of the railing.

"Nellie, Nellie!" I shouted, "Don't do that! You'll hurt yourself!"

She hollered down in an obvious drunken voice, "Just you shut your ugly lying mouth. I won't have you talkin to me like that… You all always forget me… This is my birthday too…"

I suppose Marvin had heard the breaking glass of the bottle as he came running toward where I stood. He looked up, saw Nellie, and stopped in his tracks.

"Nellie! Nellie Tromley, you get down from there right now!"

"You just shut up Marvin, you're not my boss," She hollered as she started singing again, "Happy birthday to meeee! Happy birthday to meeee! Happy dear Nel...lee! Happy birthday to meeee."

She began swaying back and forth and twisting her body in rhythm with the eerie song. She wore a pair of those low black patent shiny shoes— Mary Janes--and as we watch in dread there was nothing we could do as we both saw her left foot slip on the smooth white paint of the railing and Nellie toppled off the balcony.

It was like Marvin and I were frozen in time; I couldn't holler as I saw her fall, there was no sound from Marvin, but Nellie had started her song again as she fell from the second floor.

Marvin moved quicker than I thought the big man could. He was beneath her in a flash and caught her in his arms as she hit his chest. He collapsed from the blow of her hitting him, but sat up still holding her in his arms.

The silence was thundering in my ears, or was that my heart beating so loudly? Marvin and I finally moved and turned to look at each other. I had never seen Marvin afraid of anything, not the time some drunk tourist had threatened him with a knife, not the time a kid from Ohio had nearly drown and had stopped breathing in the pool and Marvin had dragged him out and started giving him CPR, not the time when a teenager had been so high on something he had climbed up the cherry picker Marvin uses to trim the palm trees and Marvin had talked him down, but now he was shaking.

"I think she's done for..."

Nellie moaned and opened her eyes, "You take your filthy hands off me, Nigra! I'll have you arrested and horse whipped for touching a white lady."

He put Nellie on the grass and as he stood, he placed his big hand on my shoulder and leaned against me. I was pushed back by the force and he quickly grabbed me and helped me stand upright.

"Marvin, I'm so sorry. She's drunk..."

"She's what remains of the old South. And she's drunk..."

Then he was the usual Marvin again as we turned to the crumpled form lying before us. It was a sad picture; Nellie in her grotesque childish party dress still clutching the silly tiara in her hand. The noise-maker whistle lay a few feet away.

Marvin took charge, "I'll run get a cover of some kind and you call 911."

As I punched the numbers on my cell phone, I thought how happy I was that Paul and his friends were not here.

Several days later, a very stubborn Nellie lying in Sacred Heart Hospital, talked about her family. Cathy, over in the rental office, located Nellie's niece, a lawyer over in Cordova, Alabama, that little town west of Tuscaloosa that was nearly demolished by a tornado as few years ago.

Nellie's days at La Mancha were over. No one would have to hear her yell from her balcony to get off her sidewalk. She wouldn't be following girls like Kitty when she came to give Josephine her money.

We learned Nellie was a very wealthy woman who had been estranged from her family for many years.

40

Doogs Takes Over

Coach Brown had started two-a-day summer practices the last week of July as all high school football teams in Florida were allowed to do. Even though many guys on the team had summer jobs, he was trying to run plays that the new members didn't know. Because of Paul's accident and the graduation of last year's nine seniors, he had a brand new team.

Doogs was having a hard time without Paul being there, making silly mistakes in a pass play to a wide receiver he knew very well, but he had thrown the ball to the opposite side of the receiver that the play called for two times in a row.

"Okay, gentlemen, take a water break," Coach Brown hollered.

The team ran as one to the fountain at the end of the field next to the FWB Booster club concession stand for it was a hot Florida August day and the usual Gator Ade bottles were not waiting for them.

Coach shouted, "Doogs. Come see me."

Doogs knew what he would say as he trotted back to the middle of the field where they had been running the scrimmage.

"Look, Coach, I'm so sorry. I know that play. You know I do. I'm just having a hard time concentrating."

"Why don't you ask him to come to practice?"

Doogs was stunned for a second and blurted out, "You know he won't. He's pretty lamed out about his foot and all and not being able to play."

138

"Ask him anyway."

Three days later Paul was sitting in the bleachers watching the team. He had told Doogs no about twenty times before, but when Coach Brown had called and told him that Doogs needed him there, he had gone to the next practice.

Doogs was surprised and ran up the bleachers to the top where Paul sat. He had a huge grin on his face, and exclaimed, "Thanks, man! I love you dude."

He had no idea how much that hurt Paul as he said it, but instantly realized his mistake. He looked away over the top of the bleachers and could see the Gulf in the distance as he said, "Just thanks..."

A few days later another man sat down near Paul to watch the practice also. He was a few years older than Paul, and when Coach walked by down on the field, waved and smiled, which was something he never did at a practice, he shouted, "Hey you two."

They both stood up and waved back. The guy next to Paul walked over and said, "Hey. My name is Ryan Tilley. I graduated from FWBH a few years ago, played a little football then, and wanted to see what we got this year."

Paul knew who he was before Ryan had introduced himself, "Yeah, I know who you are. I bet every guy--even all those new guys--on that field out there knows who you are."

"Well, I know who you are too. You played the game pretty well yourself."

Instantly Ryan saw that he had said the wrong thing and quickly added, "Hey, I hear you love the water about as much as I do. How about we go fishing?"

The uncle that sold Ryan his plane had a neat little fishing boat, a Triumph 185 Sportsman, and Ryan used it almost whenever he wanted to. In fact, it was tied up on the Sound most of the time in front of Ryan's house.

"Sounds like a plan, but I'll have to check with my mom."

"Okay. I have to go now. No rest for the wicked. I'll see you probably tomorrow. The team any good?"

"I think they will be, but there are a lot of newbies. See you tomorrow."

*

Later when several of us were sitting around the big Y shaped pool in front of the gazebo Trish asked, "Does anyone know Ryan Tilley?"

None of us did, but Bicycle Bob said, "Isn't that the guy who flies the plane pulling those banners?"

I started to say, "Oh, is that his last name…

But Marvin had walked up and heard Bicycle Bob ask his question, "What's up with Ryan? He's not having trouble with the plane, is he? He lives two houses down from me on the Sound. Been there about twenty years. Lived with his mother until she moved to Panama City. They moved down here to get away from the wild Spring Break bunch, but she had too many friends there, so she moved back. His dad worked for some airline, and he was on that Air Tram that crashed in the swamp north of Valparaiso."

I glanced quickly at Trish. Her bottom lip was trembling and the blood had drained from her face.

Marvin asked, "You okay, Trish?"

She replied in a monotone almost, "My husband was on that plane too."

"Oh, good Lord, Ma'am. I had no idea. I'm so sorry I have upset you."

"I know Marvin, because I know you. I'll be okay in a minute."

One of the women handed her a bottle of water; she nearly emptied it before she quit drinking.

"Now, Marvin, tell me about Ryan Tilley. He asked Paul to go fishing, and I need to know it is okay to let him go?"

Marvin cleared his throat and looked at me like I should have told him about Paul's dad, and said, "Trish, I don't think I know of a better man than Ryan Tilley unless it's Paul Bishop."

He turned around abruptly and left. We all sat in silence until Trish excused herself and headed back toward the Seagull.

41
Rig Hopping

He wanted very much to turn his cell phone back on, but he had seen that guy on NCIS pinpoint where a cell phone was operating. He reasoned that he was too expert traveling from rig to rig that he wouldn't be caught anyway so he pressed the top of the phone, Pus ran from his hand that night. He had rewrapped it first with a piece of cloth he found in an office on one of the rigs, but the medicine kit was not where it should have been and he couldn't find any antibiotics on any of the rigs since then. It was really infected he knew but he couldn't do anything about it.

A long time passed before the bitten apple appeared on the screen of his phone. He knew the connection was weak, and he was glad. All he wanted was to know what day it was. The screen came on and he saw August 3.

As he was about to turn it off, it rang. He nearly threw it over the side of the rig he was so startled. He saw it was 850 number and knew it was the Panhandle exchange. He thought, "So let them try to pinpoint me." He answered the call.

"Brantley, this is Mark Groves. I want you to bring the company helicopter in right away."

"You know I can't and I won't. I have to figure out what to do. The police are looking for me."

Groves, his boss, answered, "Yes, I know. All of us here are surprised at all this. Why don't you come on back and let us help you work it out?"

"I can't. She made me do those things. She is telling me what to do."

"Who are you talking about?"

"My mother."

"You told me several years ago that your mother had died. What do you mean she is telling you what to do?" "She talks to me. And now, she says to hang up. Bye." He pushed the button and the call ended.

"Throw it over the side, Brantley. Throw it in the water with the sword and hands."

He instinctively did as he was told.

Then she was gone and Brantley regained a semblance of sanity. He thought, it can't be the 3rd of August.

He hadn't eaten for two days so another move was necessary. He wondered when he would reach the last rig that had some kind of food on it. He wondered if he would find any more water.

Suddenly, he saw two Florida State Police copters fly over and he lost all the bravado he had about being safe. They flew circles around the rig he was on and then flew away back toward land. When they were over the horizon, he uncovered the Sikorsky, cussed it now for being so bright yellow, and took off. He flew about two miles away, sat the copter down on what he knew was another unmanned company rig and covered it carefully.

His fear turned to panic when a fishing boat anchored down by the base of the rig and the people starting fishing. He had to stay out of sight the rest of the day. He kept wondering why the noise of his landing had not caused them to be curious, but finally late in the afternoon the boat went away.

His supplies were running too low; had he eaten the last of the candy bars yesterday, or the day before, or last week? He didn't know. He had rationed them so well, he thought, but they were gone. He searched everywhere for another one, but they were gone. "You're a dumb ass, Brantley," he heard her say.

Brantley decided he didn't like talking to her anymore. He wouldn't listen, he thought. She made him turn into someone else. He did silly things when she talked to him.

He did have his two bottles of water. He took one of them, read the label which said, 'genuine spring water,' on it and laughed out loud figuring it came out of a tap somewhere, but he wished he had the nerve to open it. No, he thought, he must save it till the very end. "Drink it, Brantley. Mind me. Do it now." He opened the cap and drank the whole bottle without taking it from his lips.

He went to sleep cradling the other bottle close to him.

He jerked awake to the sound of motors. Looking over the wall of oil drums he had constructed last night he looked through the high-powered binoculars the company required him to have on the Sikorsky and saw the same two police copters circling the rig he had been on. In the early morning light he saw two other copters were with them, Alabama copters. He saw circling far outside the ring of State copters, the television copter from Mobile. Several speed boats with armed troopers were approaching the rig. He saw them as they hopped onto the ladders and started climbing up the rig.

A big urge came over him to make a run for it but he stopped. He could see four or five other rigs from where he was and he thought his odds were pretty good he was safe. He settled down but now the television copter suddenly flew straight at him and Brantley had the usual urge to pee his pants. It flew over and circled back toward the other rig where all the police were.

42

Fishing

Paul told Ryan that the fishing trip was on whenever he wanted to go. Ryan suggested the following Thursday since that was the day he didn't fly the little plane and Paul readily agreed.

Paul wanted to know what to wear and where they were going. Ryan laughed as he said he was going to wear an old pair of jeans so his legs wouldn't sunburn and maybe a white shirt and tie. Paul looked at him as if he was crazy and saw the grin on Ryan's face even though he was turned halfway away from Paul.

"Oh, I get it.... Duh!"

"Wear whatever you want, just so you're not nude!"

Paul laughed and knew from right then that Ryan would become a good friend.

"We won't go out far, about a half mile where there is an only WWII era Navy boat sunk to make a reef, and maybe we'll catch some Red Snapper and if we're really lucky a Grouper. Of course, if you would rather have Mullets, we can stay in close and seine for them."

"Ha! I'll take the Snapper and Grouper, if you don't mind."

"Ha! Yourself! We'll leave about at 4 in the morning, and I'm not kidding about that. We have to be early because there could be lots of fishermen out there.

"Okay, I'll see if my mom will bring me out to your place."

"Not necessary…I'll come down the Sound and you can meet me across Santa Rosa Blvd right across from the Seashell building. Then we'll tear out down the Bay, through Destin Pass and back out in the Gulf"

"How do you know about the La Mancha?"

"Use to be a very fine young lady living in the Seashell that caught my attention."

"Oh, I see how it is."

Paul was up and waiting for Ryan with two big ham and egg sandwiches Trish had fixed for them and an Igloo cooler with bottles of water in it along with four BLT sandwiches and a quart bag of pineapple chunks.

"Gee, I'm going to ask your mom to go next time and we'll cut out the middle man."

"Yeah, in your dreams. She wouldn't fix it if I wasn't going."

They both laughed as Paul climbed into the boat.

"This is one cool boat."

"Belongs to my uncle who lives in Navarre, but I keep it most of the time. He never fishes anymore as he is getting older, and he knows how much I love to go out there and fish."

Paul quietly said, "I use to go with my dad when we lived in Destin. We had a little twelve foot boat with an outboard motor. I was five then."

"What happened to your dad, if you don't mind me asking?"

"He was killed in a plane crash."

Ryan nearly choked on the ham and egg sandwich as he turned to Paul.

He looked away across the dark water and finally said, "My dad was too."

Both of them looked at each other for what seemed an eternity until they both turned away and were very quiet for a long time. Each of them was swallowed in his personal hurt; it was very quiet.

"You know, no one from away from here would ever believe that we would bump into each other and have this thing that hooks us together."

"They might if they knew how few people actually live in the area. My dad said he knew three men who flew on that early morning plane every day. Air Tram doesn't exist anymore you know?"

"Why was your dad on the plane?"

"My mother had gone to Atlanta the day before to see her dad who was in the hospital, and Dad had to wait till the next day because of work. Why was your dad?"

"Matt was his name. He was a pilot for American and after we moved to Destin, he would fly almost every morning to get to whatever plane he was flying out of Atlanta."

And then they started talking with each other like they were old friends trying to make up time for all the things they hadn't said to each other. Ryan wanted to know how Paul had ever gotten over his dad's death. Paul answered he hadn't. Ryan said he hadn't either and time didn't seem to make it any better.

Paul told him how he went out on his paddleboard and it was the only time of peace he ever had, except for talking with the retired teacher at the La Mancha and sitting on the low wall watching a bird which seemed so much like him. He thought about telling Ryan about Roche, but he didn't.

Ryan said he could sit on the bank of the Sound with a line in the water, never catch a thing, and listen to a blues song his dad loved so much, called Little Brother. That was his peace.

They caught seven big Red Snappers except Ryan said one of them was a Brown Snapper, but half the world didn't know the difference.

As they pulled back up on the Sound next to La Mancha, Ryan said, "You know, you are a big help to Coach Brown. He told me so. Why don't you work with some of the new guys on plays?"

"I've been thinking about that. It hurts me a lot to hobble out in front of them with this foot of mine."

"It's never going to change you know, and you'll have to go to school soon, and then everyone will know. I hope you are strong enough to answer all the questions that will be thrown at you."

"That's what Doogs said the other day. He's going to be a big help"

Ryan said he hadn't been on a paddleboard for five years, so he probably would wipe out a hundred times but he'd like to go. Paul said he had never listened to Blues.

They both had a new friend for a little while. They would only get to do each of those things; paddleboard together and sit on the wall and listen to the Blues, once.

43

The Arrow

As I descended the steps from the third floor to the ground level, I sensed someone else was around. I began my walk, as I have said, early enough so that when I turn back east the sun will be rising over Destin six miles away. Therefore, I have to start walking west before daylight and I sense this morning that I am not alone in the dark. I thought rubbish, it's just because of all the happenings and the confusion and horror of Nellie's leap and I think, "Old man, you're conjuring up things."

I wished I had stepped out on my balcony before coming down this morning because as I walked around the corner I realized there was a thick fog. All the rain we had been having this week must have filled the air with lots of moisture.

But, I continued. I walked down the ramp from the gazebo, took off my shoes, and felt the familiar cold sand between my toes. It's one of the pleasures of starting my day, feeling the sand between my toes. I glanced toward the volleyball net post and could barely see the outline of it twenty feet away, but I didn't see Jonathan L. Off scavenging for food, I imagined.

At this time of morning, shapes have a darker shade of grey than the sand of the beach and bushes up in the dunes could be concealing almost anything. We have Eastern diamondback rattlers up away from the beach, but I'm assured by Bicycle Bob that they do not get down on the sand and that they detest salt water. I always carry a ski pole I brought with me from New Mexico in spite of that assurance. It also works as a steadying device in the deep loose sand.

I was almost even with where the body washed ashore and started this horrid summer when something goes 'swish' into the sand a few feet to the right of me away from the water. I must have jumped because suddenly I find myself sitting in the sand holding the ski stick in front of me defending myself. I scramble to my feet and look around. I don't see anything unusual except I really can't see much of anything.

Convincing myself that it was a bird or crab, I continue on west. As I pass the caution sign designating the beginning of the Air Command, I hear a cough. I whirl around and don't see anything moving. I laugh at myself and continue as I always do, but am thankful it's getting daylight. Suddenly I hear a loud splash out about a hundred yards from the beach and I jump again. Then I hear the familiar cries of the dolphins and see their forms jump out of the water again. I walk on without incident for what I know is over a half mile. The fog was almost gone by this time, and I turned around to see the glory of the new day. We were always bragging about the sunrises over the Sandia Mountains in Albuquerque, but the sun rising over the horizon at the edge of the world is much more spectacular.

My glasses transition into sunglasses and I walked straight into that beauty seeing the rays glittering off the water and the bright orange outlining a bank of clouds out to the south.

As I go past the caution sign, I see something sticking in the ground in front of me about twenty feet ahead. As I get near it, I can't believe my eyes. An archery arrow is standing straight up in the sand. It isn't a kid's toy arrow but a real arrow like hunters would use in a crossbow during elk or deer season. All of a sudden, I'm scared and the hair is standing up on the back of my neck. As my grandma would have said, "I just should have stood in bed this morning!"

I'm uncertain what to do next, leave the arrow where it is or pull it up to show to Trooper Blevins when he and Morat arrive this morning. As I'm about to pull it from the sand, Kelsey and the big green John Deere tractor appear coming toward me. She is raking the sand smooth for the beach goers to have clean smooth sand. As she approaches, I wave at her and she waves back.

We have become pretty well acquainted during the three summers she has been coming to the beach to escape the hot streets of Chicago. She graduates from De Paul this coming spring so this may be her last summer with us.

I flag her down motioning for her to stop before she gets to me. She puts the tractor in neutral, gets down and walks to me, and sees the arrow.

"What in the world is that, Prof?"

"I just want you to help me build a wall of sand around it, and then if you can, stay by it while I run up and get my phone. I need to call either Trooper Blevins or Detective Morat and see if I can get one of them out here right away."

"Sure, I'll help. How did that get down here, I wonder?

You all have lots of weird things happening around the La Mancha this summer."

"Yes, we do. Help me pull sand up around it, and we'll just leave it standing inside a ring of sand."

We built a moat around it higher than the arrow and when we finished, it could not be seen over the top of the sand. I thanked Kelsey and hurried up to get my phone. When I turned and looked back at her, she was just shaking her head and tearing the foil off the first stick of gum for the day. The teacher in me disapproved and I thought, 'Why do kids torment teachers with wads of chewing gum?'

When Trooper Blevins heard my story, his first question was, "Anything else unusual happened to you recently?

Anything besides the dead body?"

"No, I did have a flat tire last week and I thought it was strange because I bought a new set of four about a month ago. It wasn't actually flat and when I got to the Toyota dealership, the mechanic said it looked like someone had driven a nail into it because the nail hadn't gone in down where the tread is but a little bit up on the side. He said sometimes that happens, so I just dismissed the whole thing."

"Anyone mad at you that you know about?"

"I don't know. Many people know I go walking early in the mornings on the beach. And, of course, I'm a retired teacher—we always have former angry students, but the last place I taught is 1300 miles away, so that's a slim possibility."

"Well, I guess we better tell Morat when he gets here, and maybe Marvin too as he is always out and about and usually knows what's going on."

"I can hardly wait to see Morat's face."

Blevins smiled, and said, "Well, you'll get your chance, because here he comes."

Something was strange about Morat's appearance this morning, stranger than usual. Then I realized what it was; he is trying to grow a mustache. I could see the beginnings of two straight horizontal lines and wondered how long he would allowed them to get beyond his cheeks.

"You found what?"

"We haven't moved it and Kelsey and I piled sand up around it without touching it."

"Good thinking." He almost sputtered as he gave me the compliment. "Let's go down and see it."

Morat has had troubles walking in the sand since he first walked out there when we found the body. He wears leather soles and they slide on the loose sand, but he will not take off his shoes to walk barefoot in the sand. He claims it's nasty.

Blevins scooped the sand back from the arrow and we all saw that it had a steel shaft with close-cropped feathers. Blevins would find out later that the shaft was really a carbon alloy, that it was very similar to arrows Olympians use and that thousands of hunters buy each year. The point was something called deep six steel field points and was deadly. Using a crossbow, the arrow became one of the hardest hitting on the market.

Morat groaned when he saw how dangerous the arrow could be, cussed in his usual unintelligible pseudo-French and when he spoke, it sounded like a squeak, "I just don't need this now...."

Blevins grinned at me, and I had to look away.

"All right, what happened this morning?" Morat demanded.

I swallowed hard, and want to shout, 'You little ass hole, I'll tell you just once, and you better listen,' but I didn't.

"It was dark and foggy when I walked down the stairs and I sensed someone was out there besides me.

"Why did you think someone was out there?"

"I just sensed it, like I have a feeling when something is going to happen. You know?"

"No, I do not. That doesn't happen to me."

I looked at him wondering what it would be like to be around him all the time, but I went on, "I walked down the slope of the gazebo, took off my shoes, turned to see if Jonathan L was on the pole—I could just make out the outline of the pole. I walked on west, heard something hit the sand with a little swishing sound, laughed at being scared, thought I heard a cough, turned around again but nothing was moving and all I could see were the shapes of bushes and vines on the dunes, so I just ignored it because I wasn't certain I heard a cough in the first place. Oh, I did hear a bunch of dolphins diving in the water. As I came back, the sun was up, I saw the arrow, Kelsey and I protected it with sand, and I called JC."

"And you didn't see anyone?"

"I will tell you this one time and if you ask me again, I'll tell you to go screw yourself. I did not see anyone. The shapes in the dunes of the grasses and bushes could have hidden anything."

Morat sputtered, but Blevins interrupted just at the right time. "Prof, I think you need to go get some of your Folgers, right now."

He nodded for me to hurry and I did.

44

Marvin Warns Me

The pelicans don't seem to know anything is amiss at the La Mancha. They flew their pass overhead this morning, and like they were showing off or showing respect, they turned and flew over again. Two of them dropped out of the formation and went skimming over the water. It looked like they were dragging their big balloon bottom jaws in the water as they went, they were so low.

Then, one of them seemed to stop in midair and plop down into the water. It was there for only a split-second as it rose, and I could see some kind of fish disappear down its throat. The other one followed suit and suddenly, the whole formation dropped down and they were all fishing back and forth not far out from the shore. They flew with such speed, and I wondered how they could see a fish, drop like rocks, catch it, and rise in just a few seconds.

Then they did something which stopped everyone on the beach as they stood and watched. The pelicans flew in concert it seemed as a line of six or eight flew over where they knew the fish were and then from another direction a line about the same in number flew from the opposite direction and another group came in from another direction. This symphony was repeated and repeated. They fished for several minutes and flew away in a cluster to the west.

I watched until they were just specks against the horizon. The Gulf is calm today; that glassy seas calm. The sky is clear of clouds except a line of grey ones far out over the water. If some artist had drawn the scene, everyone would say it was so fake. It looked unreal.

Marvin came up to my condo this morning and since I hadn't eaten anything yet, I ask him if he could eat with me. He looked really appreciative and we enjoyed English muffins with raspberry smear on them. Marvin has become a friend and ally of mine which I'm very happy about. He sat for a long time before he got to what he really came after. He wanted my word that I wouldn't ever talk about what he and I had learned at Paul's condo that day when we were cleaning it for Paul and his mom to come home. I assured him of my silence and my allegiance to Paul. He said he wasn't worried about that but that I could be in danger if I ever slipped and mentioned the zip bag to anyone. He reminded me that we have some very noisy tenants at the La Mancha.

He didn't have to tell me about the arrow, but he did, "I will level with you, Prof, all this trouble is about drugs. You told us about the Lollipop out there and somehow 'they,' whoever they are, know that. You are in real danger and someone's scared you so you will quit looking and talking. Oh, I know you won't stop doing the things you always do, so I won't even try to get you to. But be careful. Watch what's going on around you better than you do now."

Marvin left saying he would try not to worry about me so much, and I told him I would buy him a beer at Tides Inn the next time we were in there together. I don't take his concern lightly though, but I wonder what kind of danger I might encounter.

45

On the *Lollipop*

Launie sat with the binoculars held up with one hand and steadied with the other for they were very heavy for her. She knew she was in trouble because she had not slept for three nights and she was hurting inside.

She kept thinking there was something she hadn't done which was important but in her hazy mind, she couldn't remember what.

Why hadn't the shipment arrived? She had called Miami and was assured that the boat had left there three days ago. There was a storm in the Gulf, but the boat never went out too far from shore, so it should have been here by now.

Damn her luck, she thought. There was a new manager at Three Corners and she had been booted out of the top floor, so here she was sitting out in the open at the State Park and gazing at the Gulf like a damn tourist.

Launie basically hated people, even the Johns who spent so much money with her, even those other customers who drove for hours to get the crack and hard stuff who spent a lot more. She even hated the girls who faithfully worked for her.

Her cell rang and a voice said, "Thirteen." Launie knew the shipment would be dropped in the Gulf at one the next night.

So did the man sitting a hundred feet away behind a short palm pretending to read a newspaper that Launie hadn't seen in her anxiety and need, for he had hacked into Launie's phone. He did not know the exact time, but he knew what the message meant. He also had heard her conversation when she called Miami, so he knew the shipment was on the way.

On Friday night, Launie saw the delivery boat arrive again from her penthouse at the Three Corners. The new manager had called her and invited her to visit him. She had paid him well to have her top floor again.

She had no idea that her getting kicked out of the penthouse was just a ruse so that DEA agents could have time to wire the place. They had learned the signal of an incoming shipment of drugs was to be a number, but even though they had listened to her conversations with Miami many times, they still hadn't discovered what time a particular number meant.

She had a taxi waiting downstairs and as she opened the door, crawled in and slammed the back door of the taxi, she shouted hoarsely that she would pay big money to get to Pensacola as fast she he could.

They pulled up to the pier in Pensacola just before midnight. She gave the driver a roll of money and he looked surprised. He jumped out and opened the door for her.

Launie bumped the *Lollipop* into two different pilings as she rammed the yacht out of its slip and into open water. She didn't want to get lost navigating the boat out there so she followed the dark shoreline from Pensacola, on through Navarre, and landmarks became familiar as she neared Fort Walton Beach from the west. She saw the open water to the south of her and pictured in her mind about how far away the package would have been dropped. She was no good at judging the distance, she realized.

She had to get it right this time, she thought. She hadn't slept for three days. She turned the *Lollipop* to the south and headed out into the night water of the Gulf.

She wasn't the only one watching the drop-off point out there. Marvin had watched her every move, had followed her to Four Corners, and had seen her jump into the taxi. He speculated she was headed to get the *Lollipop*, and now as he scanned the water from his usual place in La Mancha's gazebo, he saw the yacht appear and turn and head out away from the beach. Marvin had been waiting for this time for over two years.

Marvin's job at the La Mancha was all a cover because drugs were being brought in and sold close by the property. Few people there knew he gave no instructions to any of the help except the help and Bette. The thought ran through his mind that he had broken some rules there letting his friend the teacher do things he shouldn't but no one knew that and it didn't matter anyway. As an undercover DEA agent, Marvin had his connection to Eglin as the government was eager to catch the drug runners who had been supplying the Panhandle.

He ran west and turned to the north just past the Air Command warning sign on the beach as he had done that morning when he encountered the Prof. He wondered why the old teacher hadn't asked him about where he had disappeared. Later, he had felt he had to warn the teacher about being quiet and he hoped he hadn't frightened him.

The land is just piles of sand and dunes, or they seem to be if you don't know where to run. Ivan had torn out the stand of scrub pine and the Air Command had never done anything about it except clean up the debris. He had a tough time in the dark getting through the dunes but he soon was on the path he had used many times in the last two years. He was challenged by a guard, but the young Petty Officer Third Class saw who he was, and saluted him smartly as Marvin ran past. Marvin grunted, and smiled. He had not been a Navy Seal for a dozen years and this kid was saluting him.

Launie couldn't find the package. She turned the yacht back and forth in the water, but since she was having a difficult time steering and watching, she was making very wide turns which almost caused the *Lollipop* to be going in circles.

159

She was getting more afraid with each minute she was out there. She could hear the big engines roaring as she turned and she realized they could be heard far away. Damn the waves, she thought, for they were continuously changing; she thought she saw something, would aim for it, and pass through nothing but a wave. They would form and look like an object only to dissolve into the water right in front of her eyes. She was trembling with a slow burning rage that she had to be out there in the first place. She pushed up on the throttle too much and she was nearly thrown overboard as she swerved and shot past the package. Or at least she thought she had seen the package as the boat sped past it.

She caught her breath and shrieked as a form bore down on the *Lollipop*. She scrambled to stand as the huge Black Beard Pirate ship slid past the *Lollipop* missing it by inches. It had looked like something from the 1800's to Launie; as it came at her she hadn't seen it but its captain had seen her. He was puzzled which way to go for the erratic movements of the *Lollipop* made no sense. He had no choice as he almost grazed the yacht. Many of the partiers on the Pirate Cruise shouted obscenities at Launie as they passed. She heard loud laughter and shortly afterward, a crew member shot the cannon across the bow the *Lollipop*. The boom echoed across the water again and again. Launie was terrified.

Almost immediately she was certain she heard the sound of music which seemed to be in surround sound because she could not determine the direction it was coming from. She struggled to her feet and flopped down in one of the chairs at the little table close to the rear of the yacht. She saw a boat headed toward her blaring "I Need a Girl."

Launie thought she saw a nude couple with all their limbs entwined about each other. As the other boat came closer, she realized her mind was not so hazy after all, as the beach boy from La Mancha and a blonde with a killer figure pulled up beside her.

He didn't seem at all ashamed to stand before her naked as he asked, "You need some help? We've been sort of watching you and wondered if you were in trouble with your boat. You almost got rammed by the Pirate Cruise."

Launie mumbled, "No, I'm fine. I dropped my expensive bag overboard, and I've been trying to find it."

The blonde, who Launie finally recognized as Sheila, one of her girls, laughed loudly as she lifted a bottle of tequila to her mouth. She chugged a long draw from the bottle and looked at Launie in a teasing way, "You want to join us? We could have some fun!"

Launie saw the young man turn red and she wondered if it were from anger or embarrassment, "No, Sweetie, I don't think I could keep up with you."

Launie remembered Kitty bragging at the Dorm about what she had done with this kid. She could readily see why. She thought Kitty was a fool to write 'SUCKER' across his windshield because all Launie needed was more attention she thought.

He jerked the wheel of the rented boat sharply and as they sped away, the blonde was having trouble standing, but Launie could hear her loud vulgar laugh. I'll have a good laugh with you later Launie thought, if you live long enough.

Launie sat in the captain's seat and gradually her breathing returned to near normal. "Damn Chuck for bringing her out in the open here. Damn him for not being here to do his job. Damn Kitty for disappearing. Just screw the whole bunch!" she almost screamed.

Startled, she regained some of her composure; she whirled the big boat around, slowed the boat and headed back. Sweat was running down her sides beneath her arms. A dark stinking stain was making rings on her expensive blouse. Launie was in bad shape… She needed some of her own product badly…

Marvin finally reached the copter pad where a HH 60G Search and Rescue choppers stood ready. He ran inside the hanger and in a matter of minutes, he and a pilot ran back out and piled into one of the choppers.

Choppers fly in and out of the Command Center all the time, so Marvin believed Launie on the *Lollipop* wouldn't be surprised or scared as they flew out. He and the pilot decided to break a rule so the chopper was flying without any lights. They decided to wait until they had nearly reached the boat and then turn on the high-powered search light.

Marvin was so close he could taste it. He had worked for almost three years to crack how drugs were getting into the Panhandle so easily. They had nearly caught a shipment out on Interstate 95 but had stopped the wrong car. He had thought for months that Launie and Chuck Jenkins were involved because they always had too much money but Launie's strip joints had been a good cover and he hadn't been able to prove anything.

Now, he knew he had her. He wanted so much to be done with this, take his wife to Tides Inn, watch his younger brother shuck about a bushel of oysters for him, and drink some beers.

Only two things could stop him now he thought; she might see them, get scared and run for it, or something else might interfere. Marvin thought of Morat and his impatience and laughed out loud at his own. The pilot heard his laugh and turned to him and smiled.

They saw the lights of the *Lollipop* as it encountered another boat and then saw it turn and head back toward Pensacola.

Marvin cussed out loud, "Damn it, she's getting away.

Tonight maybe, but not for long. Turn us around."

Marvin had no idea how true his prophecy would be for Launie had just made a decision that would catch her.

46

Money from the Banks

He didn't dare go to his regular places to eat like the Tides Inn, but went to Destin where he seldom had gone before and ate all his meals.

He was a little sorry that he had chosen the crystal red Lacrosse because it was so bright red, and then he thought it just might attract attention and people wouldn't notice him. Chuck loved the little Buick; it wasn't as heavy as the Cadillac, but it had some real power. The V6 engine made the car almost jump as he pushed the gas pedal to the floor.

He made trips to eight banks in the area the next day. He remembered the night of his twenty-third birthday when Launie had shown him the little black box as she informed him that he was on the list at the banks to enter the safe deposit boxes if anything happened to her. She had told him at the same time that if he ever thought of stealing it from her, she would throw him out. That was his mother, give him trust at one moment, and threaten to disown him in the next one. He had wondered who else was on the list and thought it might be Josephine. He knew Launie had to be taking care of her.

The first bank was the hardest because he wasn't prepared for the questions the lady had asked. Finally, after lying about his mother being sick, and giving her his real driver's license, and having the right key which was attached to each bank's name in the box he had taken from Launie, the lady took him into the room where the safe deposit boxes were.

She turned her key into the box which she had sat before him and left the room. He was nervous because he didn't know what might be in the box. He inserted his key and opened the box. It was stacked neatly with large denomination bills just like Launie always packed the boxes she mailed to Miami. Chuck loaded the bills into the rolling tote bag and relocked the box and left the room. He thanked the lady on his way out.

The next seven banks were similar experiences except one man had asked him how Launie was, and Chuck had said she wasn't feeling well. The man was a little surprised as he said he thought he had seen her walking on Santa Rosa Blvd yesterday. Chuck said he thought it might be hot flashes or something, and the man actually blushed.

And then he had nearly messed-up on the last two banks as he had removed the last two keys from the plastic cards matching them to a particular bank. He had selected the wrong key in the next to last bank, but the older lady who waited on him had said, "That's not our key, that belongs to FN Bank." Chuck had produced the correct key and she had smiled at him in a motherly way.

In that box Chuck found something much more important than money to him. He found two birth certificates sealed in a long envelope which answered a question that had haunted him for all his life, one that Launie would never talk about.

By the middle of the afternoon, he had all eight totes in the trunk and back seat of the Buick. He loaded them into the grocery cart near the elevator in the Dolphin building and took them up to his condo. He collapsed on the couch with a water glass full of Jack and 7Up!

47

Streaked

Brantley was laughing uncontrollably as he slapped the dull grey paint on the Sikorsky. The part of Brantley who had never been a kid because he hadn't been allowed to be one, outlined a big fat horse on the door of the copter and then filled it in with his hands. Then he smeared the paint around and around. He had to be careful and not get paint on the motor.

From his confused mind he realized he was ruining one of his three prized possessions. That other part of him took his left hand and jerked the right one back and slapped it against the side of the copter. Blood and pus and the grey paint started running down Brantley's arm as he screamed in pain.

He yelled the dirtiest word he knew, "Piss on it. Just damn piss on it."

He had found the large container of deck paint and thought he could hide the bright yellow Sikorsky by camouflaging it. On the same deck he had found a container of raw crude oil. Now the Sikorsky stood covered with streaks of the grey paint and globs of the sticky oil.

He fell back flat on the deck and starting crying and yelling like an insane person as he realized what he had just done.

She was there all of a sudden and lashed out at him, "You're a pee-pee baby, Brantley. You just destroyed the one thing which kept you halfway sane. You're not a man, Brantley. Look at you…"

Brantley curled up sobbing as he fell asleep.

When he awoke several hours later the sun was starting to appear over the east horizon. The grey paint had dried over much of his face and arms. His right index finger was throbbing with every beat of his heart—it was huge and bright purple and runny with bloody pus. His clothes were covered with paint and blood and the sticky oil. Smears of the oil streaked the grey paint on his face.

He shuddered when he saw the copter. It was sitting out in the open. He had gone to sleep and left it out where anyone could see it, but he saw it would be hard to see it from a distance. He smiled and thought Ryan would say he had his stuff together this morning. He was relieved to see that the blades and rotor were untouched. He thought it would still fly.

48

A Horrific Day on 98

Hurricane Ivan ripped through the strip of Highway 98 between the two bridges; Brooks Bridge which humps up over the Sound at Fort Walton Beach and swoops downward to the stoplight at the east end where you turn right for Okaloosa Island, and the Pass Bridge six miles on east which humps up over the pass from the Bay out into the Gulf of Mexico. Ivan nearly cut the Gulf into the bay, but not quite.

Nearly all the dunes on both sides of the highway were leveled and much of the road was destroyed. The pine groves and scrub thickets were thrown over into the Bay or stripped bare. Even today, after almost ten years, only a few lonely pines still stand on the Bay side. The scene is surreal as some of the old trees which may be thirty to forty feet tall are dead alien gray spikes pointing skyward like barbaric spears from science fiction horror. They stand jutting upward out of the new green grown. Others which are still living are nude most of the way up their trunks. They have a washbowl haircut of branches clustered at the tops.

Many months after Ivan hit, the road reopened again after being reinforced with tons and tons of large rocks which would let the surge of water from the next big wind seep through it the engineers hoped.

It is smooth, flat for the six miles, and nearly straight. Traffic travels fast on it—cars whiz along oblivious of the 55 mph speed limit. When I drive over to Destin, I get the feeling that the road is lower than the Bay on the north side, but I'm told that it's not. The road runs closer to the Bay side and certainly looks lower than the shallow water of the Bay.

Islands break through the surface of Choctawhatchee Bay when the tide pulls the water back out into the Gulf. Crab Island, just to the north of the Pass Bridge, is one of the most popular tourist attractions where hundreds of boats of all kinds anchor in the water. Locals, as well as the thousands of vacationers can walk around when the tide is out. All kinds of attractions and our version of lunch trucks, pontoon boats with all kinds of food for sale—mainly seafood though--anchor out there during the summer months.

Several pull-offs on the Gulf side of the road are filled with parked cars belonging to people who walk the paths down to the Gulf as the entire six miles is owned by the government and is open to the public. It's a dangerous stretch because of all the cars entering and exiting the road and because it is straight and traffic is fast.

During the last summer weeks close to Labor Day, thousands of people fill the area along the coast of Florida from Panama City to the east, on to Destin, then to Fort Walton Beach, Navarre, and on over to Pensacola. Families with kids almost ready to return to school and college crowds getting to the beaches for one last time before the fall semester fill the towns and beaches.

On that Monday afternoon, a large group of college guys from over in Louisiana parked their cars and trucks and walked down a path to the Gulf. They pulled off in front of what Ivan had left of the Matterhorn, the largest and tallest sand dune on the Gulf Coast. Once well over a hundred and fifty feet tall school kids would ride their plastic dish sleds down it in the winter since we seldom had any snow. Ivan had demolished it to a twenty to thirty foot tall pile of sand blowing the rest over onto the Bay side of the road or clear over into the Bay itself.

The fraternity guys stayed well past dark with plans to drive the entire way home in a caravan. They had too much to drink during the afternoon and evening and when their illegal bonfire burned down to embers, they worked their way back up the path and loaded into their cars and trucks.

All semblance of responsibility disappeared as they drove their vehicles squealing out into 98 trying to see who would be the first leader of the caravan. A big Hummer shot out into the road across the median and into the outer west bound lane. It broadsided a little 1986 red Volkswagen.

Paul and Roche were returning from a youth party at Henderson State Beach Park in Destin. Forty or so young people had gathered to roasted hotdogs and marshmallows to make S'mores, and to sing songs. The youth pastor, a little short man with a goatee, a real motivator had talked with them about the upcoming year at school and how they might get involved with activities.

They loaded their things and since Paul had trouble shifting, Roche always drove when they went somewhere in her little car. They crossed the Pass Bridge, saw the huge crowds and hundreds of boats on Crab Island, and were about a mile on Highway 98 when the Hummer shot out into the road.

Six or more cars collided into a tangled mass of twisted metal. Tires torn loose from vehicles rolled down the road causing a pile-up of traffic that the Okaloosa deputies said was at least twenty cars. Roche's little car seemed to have hit a wall, then abruptly sailed into the air and landed in a crumpled tangled pile way off the road among the sand dunes close to the Bay.

All four lanes of 98 rapidly filled and traffic came to a standstill from Brooks Bridge to the Pass Bridge. The ER vehicle with its horn blasting and siren wailing inched its way through the stopped cars. Several times it left the road onto the median or treacherous sand along the side in danger of getting stuck. It was going east from the fire station on Santa Rosa Blvd at FWB almost five miles from the accident; many cars did pull off the road to let it past but others didn't as the drivers saw so many other cars sink into the sand.

Thirty minutes went by before it reached the collision. The jaws-of-life operator worked long into the night to get them out of the wreck. Traffic was still stopped at the massive pile-up which lit up the night with flashing lights and the fires of two burning cars when Paul and Roche were loaded into the ambulance. Finally it worked its way across the Pass Bridge wailing away through Destin to Mercy Hospital with the bodies.

Paul and Roche were dead.

49

Prospecting on the Beach

Ollie was terrified more than he had ever been except when the Yellow dog had ripped his leg open as he hung from the fire escape trying to escape the water of Katrina.

And now Launie had sat him out near Angler's Pier with a silly looking device which he certainly didn't know how to operate, but that she had told him to carry just so and to turn the red light on. She had bought him a hat with a green band which he was delighted with. She told him that he was to look for a package about the size of his shoe box and bring it right to her if he found it. She warned him to keep moving the long handle of the device she had given him back and forth across the sand, but to watch all around him for the box. She told him under no circumstances was he to go beyond the red sign that he would see.

Ollie was scared as he walked, but no one seemed to pay attention to him. He had never been on this beach before. He didn't want to get the sand between his toes. It felt nasty to him like chicken-shit he had stepped in once. As he looked down the beach, he saw all kinds of people that he had never noticed before.

Up ahead was another man with a device like the one Launie had given him this morning. The man was moving it back and forth along the sand, so Ollie started copying him. When the two of them were side by side, the other man asked if he had found anything, and Ollie said no, but that he was looking for the box. The other man looked at him with a strange look.

He saw two small children who were filling plastic buckets with sand and carrying them to where they were building a castle. Ollie was intrigued and walked toward them. They stopped and stared at him and when he offered to carry sand for them, they agreed. About an hour later they had a large but crude castle built several feet from the shoreline. The little boy took a bucket and ran to the water, brought it back and poured water in the moat they had created. Ollie was delighted. For the next half hour he carried bucket after bucket of water for the moat.

Grown-ups sitting in Max's chairs or lying on towels on the sand became concerned that Ollie was getting too involved with the two children. One lady asked if he was their uncle, and he shook his head back and forth several times.

Then Ollie sat on the sand and created a huge arrow which looked distinctly like the ones he had in his arsenal. The father of the two children walked over and took them away. Ollie was disappointed and anger started building up inside him. He kicked the castle into a pile of sand, fell on his knees and scoop big hands full of sand into the moat.

He destroyed all they had built except the arrow. Several people moved from the area where he was, and the father went to talk to Max about the strange man who had just turned 'dangerous' he said.

Ollie knew enough to leave and started walking west again, saw the red sign, and was relieved that he could turn around and go back. He saw a brown box wrapped in burlap sticking up out of the sand just beyond the sign. He hesitated because he had been told to not go past the sign. But Ollie made a decision, stepped past the sign, pulled the box out of the sand, and started walking back east.

Now everyone was staring at him. Max started toward him, saw who he was, turned and walked away.

Ollie came to the ramp, hesitated and then turned to walk up to the gazebo; his instinct told him it was the way out to Santa Rosa Blvd. As he left the gazebo and was walking down the walk, a little dog stuck its head through the railing of one of the balconies and starting barking furiously at Ollie. Ollie threw the metal detector into the lawn and ran for the parking lot as fast as he could. He was terrified and furious.

Launie had been driving up and down the Blvd for almost two hours wondering what had happened to Ollie when she saw him emerge from the lane at the entrance of La Mancha. She pulled up beside him and began to praise him when she saw he had the box. Her need for the stuff in the box caused her to speed all the way down the Blvd and go through a yellow light at 98. She parked behind the Dorm and rushed inside with the box.

Ollie went to his rooms behind the Dorm, dressed in his full Green Arrow uniform—the plaid green shirt and faded jeans, fitted the night-vision goggles around his neck, armed himself with as many quivers of arrows as he could and started out down the Blvd. He had studied hard while they had just driven up it to remember where to go.

The first shots Ollie took were at the tires of the fire trucks at the station just across Highway 98. He beamed with glee as he saw three tires deflate to the ground.

He ran down the Blvd nearly getting hit by a pickup truck as he paid no attention to the traffic. He turned in anger and shot several arrows into the approaching traffic. Several cars swerved into a low ditch by the road there and two crashed into each other. By this time Ollie was excited more than he could remember as he started running. He shot out all six windows at the Tom Thumb as he went by.

Then he stopped and decided he didn't want to play anymore. He headed north on one of the side streets and wound his way back up behind Tides Inn, slipped across the 98, and disappeared down the drainage ditch to his fort.

J C and the Okaloosa County deputies conducted a house to house search far into the night, but no one seemed to know who they were looking for. Scores of people described the spectacle from as many points of view, but none had seen where he had gone as they were all hiding. The descriptions varied from a young kid with a mask to a man with a crossbow.

Ollie had escaped.

Max knew who Ollie was, but he wasn't talking

50

Part of the Water

Paul and his mother were Lutherans and still belonged and went every Sunday to Faith Lutheran in Destin. Trish and I convinced the Owners Association that Paul's funeral could be on our beach front. We had had many weddings on the beach in front of the gazebo, but never a funeral that I know about.

After all the horror that had happened there in the last few weeks, we tried at first to persuade Trish to not have the funeral there, but she told me if anyone knows how he loved the Gulf, it surely was me. We all did our best to help her with the service for she looked like she might need medical help herself before this was all over.

Gerald, the guard at our little entrance shack, finally put a sign on the window that the security guard was out walking the property and the hundreds of cars hesitated, the drivers read the sign, and then entered the property. The parking lots filled and both sides of the Blvd had cars parked by the sides far down toward Highway 98. So many people had never been to the La Mancha at one time.

I saw many of the same people who had been at the more traditional funeral yesterday when all her friends had worn a pink rose in their hair or pinned to a shirt. Faith Church had put extra chairs down the three aisles, the choir loft was full as well as the balcony, and people had stood in the lobby. Roche had so many friends....

Youth Pastor Greg Stone, a little bald man with a voice which carried out over the crowd paused in his talk in rhythm to the waves. As I realized his concert with the waves, tears filled my eyes as I thought Paul would smile. Pastor Greg stood in the gazebo and talked about a young

176

kid who took on the responsibilities of a man far too early because of his father's death. He talked about Paul being a leader, not only on the football field at FWBH but in the classroom and at his church.

He looked out to the hundreds who were gathered; young kids from Destin and FWBH, nearly every full-time resident of La Mancha, all Paul's teachers and the administration of his school, Roche's family, and Doogs. I sat by Trish in what I suppose were the only two chairs on the beach. No one saw the man standing on the balcony of Condo 63 watching.

We all stood shoulder to shoulder to sing and I saw many faces strained with sorrow. A young man, older than high school students, I thought, came up and stood beside me. I turned to look at him and he held out his hand, "I'm Ryan."

I held my hand out to him, and said, "Yes, you would be. Paul thought the world of you."

"And I did him too," his voice broke into almost a whimper as he rapidly blinked his eyes.

All I could think about was that silhouette of Paul in the afternoon sun riding his board out into the water. "You must come and visit me."

"I would like that," he stammered.

Pastor Greg led the singing with a very old song I learned years ago, "Shall We Gather at the River?" but he had us substitute 'Water' for 'River.' As the crowd started to sing that old hymn, I swear a lone seagull flew over and went high into the afternoon sky. I wouldn't even imagine it was Jonathan L, but Paul would like that I thought it was.

Trish had had Paul cremated and Pastor Greg held up the little jar which contained his ashes, took Trish by the arm and they walked down to the shore. The crowd parted before them, and at the water's edge Doogs was waiting with Paul's long board.

Trish seemed to stumble and dropped the little jar. There were several little exclamations from those who had seen it but some of us knew that it had to be planned.

We knew it was against all laws to be doing what was happening. She and Pastor Greg squatted down and gathered up the ashes mixed with the sand. They walked to the water's edge and sprinkled Paul's ashes on his board.

Although he was shaking so much he could hardly stand, Doogs waded out into the Gulf pushing Paul's board in front of him. He went out about a hundred yards, let the board go and it came skimming parallel across a line of waves headed back into shore.

Paul would never leave the waters he loved so much.

Doogs retrieved the board when he made his way back to shore, stood it on its end and stood there with tears streaming down his cheeks.

51

What to do with the Money?

Chuck had watched Paul's funeral from his balcony with just as much attention as that day when he watched Joe's body laying out there. He admired Paul for the honest decent kid he was. He thought many times how much Paul and Trish loved each other; sometimes he was bitter when he thought of Joe and him and Launie.

Chuck didn't want the money; he wanted revenge for how she had treated them and especially for how she had reacted to Joe's death. Now that he had it, he had to decide what to do with it.

There were bills of almost every denomination except ones and fives. He thought how strange, as he looked at the stack of $2 bills. The biggest concern he had were the big Federal Reserve Notes which Chuck did not know how to cash; there were 52 of them. How or where Launie got them would remain a mystery he knew. They had been out of circulation for many years and they totaled $360,000; he had no idea what he would do with them, but suddenly a solution entered his mind.

He knew that collectors would jump at the chance to have the big bills. But he had no doubt that whoever ended up with them would have to use some skill in getting the most possible for them, and it would undoubtedly be a long tedious process to sell them.

Big stacks of fifties, hundreds, and $500 bills lay on the bed also. After almost two hours, he had what he thought was a grand total for all the money except the $360,000 and those silly $2 bills. He was not expecting so much, $6,585,750 dollars.

What the hell will I do with all this, he thought.

But Chuck was not like his mother, and several possibilities ran through his mind.

52
More Arrows

Max has certainly changed as I see him constantly looking around when he first arrives in the mornings. I haven't seen Marvin around the property at all. Kelsey seems to be the only one who acts just as she always had, but then, she is not really involved with the La Mancha. After Morat questioned her and she told him to take what she said or just leave her alone, I guess she is back in her daily routine.

I sleep with the sliding patio door to my bedroom open each night with just the screen closed. I enjoy the splashing of the waves because they are continuously changing.

Last night I heard someone whistling down below on the lawn. It was a whistle like someone was trying to get the attention of someone. There are still many tourists here right now that I didn't think anything about it, and since I hadn't slept much this week, I turned over and the waves and rain that was falling steadily soon put me back to sleep.

When I got up this morning, turned my coffee machine on, and went to brush my teeth, I heard the yard men down below cussing at something.

"Son of a Bitch... Would you believe that? How did that happen?" the taller of the two exclaimed. Andy is known for his redneck humor and foul mouth.

"How would I know?" the shorter one asked.

I hurried brushing my teeth, went to the kitchen to get my mug of Folgers, and walked out onto my balcony. There are three palms trees out about a hundred feet almost directly in front of my condo; their tops come up almost even with the floor of my balcony.

As I looked down at them this morning, I had to sit down in one of my pub chairs. All three of the trees had arrows sticking out of their trunks about ten to fifteen feet from the ground. Not just one arrow in each tree, but what looked like a dozen or more in each, and shot at them from different directions.

All at once, I had no desire for my coffee. I looked around and started to go inside as Marvin came around the corner and hollered to ask if I would call Blevins.

Blevins couldn't believe what I was saying. He said he would be right out.

By the time he arrived, twenty or so people were standing around looking at the trees. One little boy hollered that he wanted an arrow and ran toward the trees. His dad grabbed him and pulled him back. Marvin and his two men paid more attention to the crowd then and formed a circle at the foot of the palms.

When Blevins arrived, I walked down and was standing with them by the pool fence. He asked, "Did you hear anything during the night?"

"No, as you know it's been raining pretty hard for the last four or five hours and I sleep like a baby when it rains, so I was fast asleep. No, that's not exactly true, I heard someone whistling. Sounded like it was down on the lawn right below me."

"Well, we may be jumping to conclusions that these incidents are aimed at you. You were on the beach, but that arrow might have been to get our attention or just some kid out having an adventure in the dark. These here might just be because we're standing in the most public place on the complex."

181

"Seems like a pretty definite warning at me, if you ask me."

"I'm not saying it isn't, I'm just saying we don't know that."

One of the palms is right next to the low perimeter fence which means that from the other side of it, the shooter would have to be on the beach or in the dune between the fence and the beach. Marvin went down to investigate, but came back saying that the rain had washed away any footprints which may have been there.

Morat arrived and his first question was, "Have you seen any suspicious cars around?"

By this time, Blevins, Marvin, and I know not to look toward each other when he asks a question like that—a "Morat" question--or we might laugh in his face.

I replied, "You might want to go door to door and see if anyone has."

Blevins cleared his throat loudly and said, "There is no way to know where these arrows were bought. It could be anywhere in the country, on Amazon, or a Bass Pro. We don't have any reason to start checking stores around here, because I would bet they were bought far away."

Morat blurted out, "Wouldn't hurt to send the deputies around and ask."

"Well, you're in charge of them, and if that's what you want to do, go ahead. But, I say all we can do is wait for the next event to happen."

Marvin was really upset when he saw the destruction to the palms. Palms are not indigenous to the Panhandle. Thousands have been brought into the area and each is planted carefully and must be nourished and sprayed for disease on a regular basis. I have no idea what one costs, but these three will probably have to be dug up and new ones planted.

Morat was right about one thing though; how in the world could that many arrows have been shot and no one in the whole complex had seen it? How long did it take to shoot all those arrows? Surely the archer must have missed his targets at least a few times, and had to recover the arrows. Those palm trees are as big around as the average man, so he had to have missed them at least some of the time. Then it occurred to me; is there more than one person doing this?

Blevins was right also. What could either of them possibly do? Everyone would just have to wait until something else occurred. Marvin told us all that he and the whole security squad would be watching the next few nights.

But the next morning, it was obvious that they had missed whoever taped the notice to my door. When I opened it to get the *NorthWest Daily*, there it was taped with a piece of duct tape. I almost grabbed it, but realized I should not touch it. I got my cell phone and called Blevins realizing that Morat would be mad at me.

When Blevins arrived he was pretty put out that Morat hadn't put anyone on patrol last night and even with all the lights on the porch of the Pelican, someone had taped the notice on my door. He pulled the notice off and came in and sat down at my table. I joined him and he opened the folded piece of paper. It was put together with words cut out of the *Daily*. It said:

Now you can see how to not be able to do what you want to do. You heard couff on the beach—you were bein watched. That time I just out having fun. You should heard the whistling—you condo is known. I after you. Have you walked around. the La Mancha and not known you were not alone?

The words must have come from several papers as we doubted they could have been found in one copy—the *Daily* is usually thin, and a few other words had been handwritten crudely into the note.

183

Blevins looked at me, "Gee, Prof, this is not good. Morat would say who is mad at you? But I won't because that's a Morat question. But, you have to take some time and really think about who is. That first line is obvious a warning of revenge."

"J C, I've had dealings with well over 4,000 students, all their parents, other teachers and administrations during the forty-two years I taught school. I've lived in four different towns and been involved in many organizations. So, how am I to know who I obviously made angry or hurt in some way? I feel like a sitting duck though."

"We've got to get you away from here. I suggest you go to your daughter's in Destin for a while."

"No sir. I will not endanger them or their property. I'll find some apartment somewhere. No, damn it, I'm not running. The person or persons obviously know where I am, probably know my car, and have been following me for some time. If I'm in danger, I have been for a while. So, why run now?"

"We'll put some kind of security watching you. I've got a young man who lives just across the Sound from here. He will come over during the nights and be here early in the mornings when whoever it is will expect you to take your morning walks."

"How long can that last? It didn't work last night. No, I've made up my mind. I'm not changing a thing. I'm not trying to be a hero or anything, but it doesn't make sense to hide and having someone watch me day and night just won't work." I reached over and picked up the notice, looked at it, and smiled. It was an amateur trick, I thought, to make us think the writer of it was illiterate.

53

Brantley's Secret Discovered

After weeks of arguing before Judge Jeffrey Bickel that when Brantley sat the Sikorsky down and took right off again he must be hiding something, Morat finally got his warrant. Marvin let them into Brantley's condo. J C entered first as Morat stood on the sidewalk unwrapping a chocolate kiss. J C nearly puked at the smell; a strong smell of bleach filled the air, but beneath that a sickening sweet smell of perfume permeated the whole place, and still beneath that was still another very unpleasant odor.

They hurried to get out after opening the front door and the sliding patio door which created a draft pulling the air out the patio door. After more than an hour, Morat led the way into the condo. Nothing seemed to be out of order. Brantley would have cleaned it up, Morat thought. But when J C went into one of the bedrooms, he came rushing back gagging. He ran out the patio door and threw up on the lawn.

Morat smiled and thought what a wimp as he walked into that bedroom. J C had taken a key off the hook on the door and opened the big floor-to-ceiling wardrobe and the door was still open. Inside was the third body. Either she had hanged herself and the door had been locked and it closed on her or someone had put a belt around her neck and put it around the rod that ran across the top. She hung there dangling in the air.

Her skin was completely dried and looked like shriveled up leather. J C said that must mean she has been in there for several years if she dried out in our humid climate.

She was dressed in an old-fashioned dress and perched on her head was a strange Pith Helmet painted with flowers all around. My God, Morat thought as he remembered the Prof describing what Brantley wore around the complex every day. On the front of the Pith Helmet were the words, "Happy Mother's Day!" On the floor of the wardrobe were dried up flowers which had been yellow Morat thought.

As he stared at the grisly mummified body in the wardrobe, a breeze from both doors being open must have caused the body to move for all of a sudden she seemed to be waving at Morat. The dried flowers skittered across the floor in front of him. Her mouth was agape as if she had just screamed something and now she was moving. She had been shut up in there alive.

Morat couldn't get out quickly enough but as he backed out of the room he saw a Bible on a table opened to where a page had been ripped out. He almost made it across the living room toward the patio door before he lost his breakfast.

When they finally returned inside both wearing those masks that look like surgical masks, Morat found the Piggly Wiggly bags under the kitchen sink where they looked like someone had stuffed them in a hurry. He found the roll of ribbon that matched the ribbon on the dead body on the beach and a pair of pinking shears lying on the floor. Here was the proof he needed to convict Brantley. Now, if only he could somehow capture Brantley alive, he might find out who the body that washed up on the beach was.

J C called Morat's attention to the outline of a missing sword that had been on the wall. Its outline was clear on the faded wall among the other swords.

Later the forensic team told Morat there seemed to be no damage to the shrunken body and that she had probably died from smothering in that tight space. They detected the presence of blood inside the shower and on the bed sheets in the washer in the laundry room where someone had washed them in what smelled like pure bleach. There had been two types of blood in the shower and one of the types was found on the door of the wardrobe.

Blevins supervised the handling of the evidence having all of it securely bagged and labeled and sent it to the State Forensic Lab. Again, Morat would have to wait, and he did very impatiently.

54
Flying with Mother

"Fly to me… Come home…"

Brantley hadn't eaten for three days and the last bottle of water was gone. Fear was taking over his mind. He saw her standing next to the Sikorsky.

He had been in total charge weeks ago when he touched down with the three company men and had taken off again to their amazement. Even flying during the day time was not dangerous for him for word of what had happened at La Mancha had not reached the rigs. After word got out, he noticed groups of men standing looking up at him as he flew over a rig. His imagination turned their gazing into some kind of admiration. "They've turned me into a hero!" he shouted as he passed over a rig one day.

The big storm we had on the Gulf the weekend of July 4th had nearly wiped him out as he was attempting a landing on a rig far outside the perimeter he knew. One shoe of the Sikorsky had slid off the edge of the landing deck; it took all of Brantley's ability to right the copter just before it crashed into the Gulf.

He became unsure about which rigs were unmanned now and had sat down on one that had a crew on it; several men had rushed toward him and he had barely escaped by taking off immediately.

The bright yellow Sikorsky became a beacon to those hunting him he knew and he had desecrated it with the paint and oil. He felt bitter about the paint for now it looked like a bird that had been caught in that horrible oil spill. But he felt better about his chances of hiding it.

During the daylight hours when he saw other copters headed toward whatever rig he had run to the night before, his thoughts were rational. He was terrified of being caught, but he knew he could see whatever was coming and hide from it.

He was lucky finding food at the beginning, but now weeks later he thought he might have found all he probably would. He was hungry, but he was really thirsty.

He stood with his feet planted firmly and shouted, "I will not go back to torture again." He shook uncontrollably as he thought about the times she had opened the door and pushed him in. He could push against the inside of the door as much as he could when he imagined the key turning in the lock. He pictured her hanging the key on the hook on the door, the key that he had never dared to touch. Since he had locked her in for some of her own medicine, he had opened the wardrobe just once.

After being gone for three weeks Brantley had returned to La Mancha to find us all really angry with him. His plan of the Grouper covering the stench of his mother did not go as he had planned. Alex, the pest-control man who regularly sprays the insides of all our condos, had opened Brantley's door four days after Brantley had left the Grouper in the refrigerator. Even though some of us had already smelled the putrid smell and a little girl at the pool had asked her dad, "I smell something dying. What is that smell?"

"I don't know Princess, but it sure stinks."

We hadn't figured out where it was coming from.

Alex didn't go into the condo because the sickening smell stopped him, but Marvin did after Alex fetched him. The Grouper was filled with maggots and it took days for the putrid smell of dead rotting fish to get out of the condo after Marvin and his crew had taken out the refrigerator and left all the windows and doors open.

"What the hell were you thinking?" Marvin yelled at Brantley when he came back.

"I only intended to be gone until the next day but when I got to Mobile, there was an emergency on a rig and I was out there until yesterday. I completely forgot about the Grouper or I would have called you. I had no idea it would cause the door to pop open."

"That was the weirdest stinking fish I have ever smelt. Didn't smell anything like a fish. That place of yours still stinks. We might not have known where it was coming from for three weeks if Alex hadn't come to spray for bugs."

Brantley instinctively shook a little as he thought. What else did Alex see or smell? He quickly covered his fear, "I apologize. Guess I'll have to buy another refrigerator."

"You're damn lucky that's all you have to do."

Brantley had apologized several more times to Marvin and to Bette, the manager of La Mancha, about how careless he had been to not know the Grouper was so large it would press up against the inside of the door and open the refrigerator.

Finally, he was back on good graces at La Mancha, but he worried that Alex or someone else had smelled that other smell that he still smelled.

He hadn't hurt her, he couldn't have done that. He was too afraid of her. She had just been sick… And she died… He put her in the wardrobe, locked the door, and hung the key on the hook… He hadn't heard her screaming for the wardrobe was nearly sound proof… That's the way it had happened in Brantley's mind…

For the next two years he lived with her. He talked with her each day and polished the wardrobe with Pledge.

And now they were after him, and she was calling him home. Last night he had seen her walking out on the waves of the Gulf beckoning him toward the La Mancha.

He decided he would fly back to the first rig he had been on as he thought it would be unlikely they would search there again. His finger hurt like hell, was twice as large as it should have been, and he couldn't keep the pus from seeping out of the ragged bandages that were all he had been able to find. His whole arm ached and throbbed and was lined with hot red streaks. It had bled on his chest as he slept last night, a dark black blood filled with watery yellow pus. As he flew toward that first rig in the darkness of the night, his mom sat in the seat next to him.

"Fly me home. Fly me there now…"

55
Attack

Mylee stood waist deep in the predawn surf covered from head to toe in heavy dark clothing as she did any time she was fishing. Waist deep is not very deep as she had struggled to get over the little perimeter fence of La Mancha for she was not much taller than it.

Almost every morning, Mylee guided her little boat with its trolling motor across the Sound and tied it up at Judge Jeffrey Bickel's dock. Not many days went by unless she left the Judge a nice fish at the day's end.

Everyone knew she crawled over the fence whenever she went fishing but no one had ever told her she was welcome to be there, so she continued day after day to sneak into the grounds of the complex.

Many mornings in the past she had seen her friend the Prof as she crossed the lawn but he had always looked the other way. She liked him very much for he had been the first to buy a fish from her and had obviously told many others because now she had a good business just selling her daily catch at the La Mancha.

She had been momentarily frightened this morning as she climbed over the fence because she saw a man standing under the portico of the Pelican where the Prof lived. The she realized it was that nice young man, David, who lived a few doors down the street from her with his wife and new daughter. They have three young ones now, she thought. He was a lawman of some kind, she knew.

She glanced his way and he was looking straight at her and called softly, "Good morning, ma'am, hope you catch a bunch this morning."

Mylee was delighted at his good manners and replied, "If I do, I'll take something nice to your wife."

"Be careful, it's very foggy this morning."

"Then the fish won't see me! Thank you, I will."

She went west of the gazebo toward the Air Command fence. The water was very cold on her legs as she cast her line out as far as her little arms let her. She started back to the shore about twenty feet away as she heard the sound of someone approaching from the east. In the foggy dark, she was worried that her small form would not be seen and she might frighten whoever it was.

She could make out the shape of the man but his face was strange; his head didn't appear to be human as the outline of his eyes seemed to bug out several inches. It was night goggles she realized like the ones she saw on soldiers when she was a little girl in Vietnam.

At almost the same time, she saw the lights go on in what she knew was the Prof's condo. A few minutes past, the balcony door slid open, and her friend sat down in one of the high chairs that she had sat in one day when he invited her up for tea. His little dog Skipper barked at something as he stuck his head through the railing.

She turned back to see the man a few yards from her and was horrified as she saw the crossbow aimed at the Prof. Just as she screamed her faint cry into the noise of the surf, the light was clear enough for her to see the arrow flying straight at the balcony. She heard the first one hit, heard the cry of pain from the Prof, and almost immediately she saw the second one hit and bring a loud yelp from Skipper.

The man shouted, "Yeah! That'll teach him. Yapping Bastard," and he turned and ran back east toward Angler's Pier.

Mylee struggle to get out of the water. Her legs wouldn't move, she thought. It seemed forever until she was running up the wooden ramp to the gazebo a few yards away. She screamed as she ran all the way and saw several lights coming on in various condos. David ran around the corner of the Pelican and met her just as she turned running toward him down the walk.

"The Prof has been hit by an arrow. I saw it all. Hurry, hurry, we must hurry."

The elevator took forever to get to the third floor. They ran down the porch and David opened the condo with his key and Mylee wondered why he had a key. But they hurried to the balcony. As David slid the door open, they heard the crying.

He was sitting on the balcony floor holding Skipper in his arms. Prof had an arrow sticking out of his right hand and the little dog was covered with blood. He sat rocking back and forth holding the little dog who had become his constant companion.

"Prof, are you hurt?" David asked.

Through the tears, he whispered, "I'm okay, but look what they have done. A poor helpless little dog that was joy to be around. A poor little thing that never hurt anything."

Mylee knelt beside him and looked at his hand. "We must get you to hospital. That arrow will be a mess to get out of your hand."

She raised his hand from where it lay on his thigh and the blood rushed from the two holes on either side. The arrow point had gone all the way through his hand and was sticking out one side while the feather end stuck out the other. He looked at it in surprise and fainted.

56

Mylee Saves the Day

I woke up in Sacred Heart Hospital the next morning to find Marvin and Trooper Blevins sitting in the two chairs outside my door. When the nurse answered my call button, they both realized I was awake.

She did the usual things of taking my temperature and blood pressure and poking and asking, "And how are we today?" I wanted to answer that I didn't feel too damn good but I had no idea how she felt, but decided to be polite. As she left, I heard her say, "Okay, you two can go in, but don't you get him excited."

J C and Marvin, both large men, filled my room and both started talking at the same time. I laughed out loud at them and stopped them with, "What did you do with Skipper?"

J C pushed my bed over to the window and down below was my friend, Sally, from the sixth floor. In her arms Skipper was squirming to be put down on the ground; he doesn't even like for me to hold him. There was a large white bandage on his left ear, but other than that he was his usual ornery self. I guess tears filled my eyes because Marvin, cleared his throat, and said that Skipper had lost part of his ear, but everything else was fine.

"What about all that blood that was on him?" I asked.

"It was yours."

I smiled and noticed for the first time that my right hand was three times its usual size and wrapped in heavy gauze. As I tried to squeeze it into a fist, a horrific pain shot all the way up to my elbow. I wouldn't be doing that again.

We heard a slight sound at the door and turned to see Mylee carrying a steaming pot of her delicious tea. She entered the room in her quiet dignity and excused herself for interrupting our meeting. J C assured her she was welcome and that he certainly wanted to talk to her.

"And I surely can't get any Folgers in this broken-down place." I joked. "Besides I would rather have your tea."

She smiled and gave me the look that she knew I was pulling her leg. She poured us tea in the plastic glasses from the restroom and was very embarrassed she had not brought her teacups with her.

J C asked her to sit down and tell us all what she had seen yesterday morning. She hesitated at first but got the jest of things in her mind and told us very clearly.

"The man was wearing night goggles. He was really carrying many arrows to go in the crossbow he was shooting." I heard what he said, but I am ashamed to say it.

J C told her, "It's all right. We will know that it's not you talking."

"Yes, but it's about the Prof, I guess. And it is not nice."

I looked at her and said, "Go ahead, Mylee. I'll understand."

"He said, that will teach you and called you a Bastard." She turned away and busied herself with the tea pot.

J C told her she had done a good job and was a big help. Then he asked if she saw anyone else and where did the man go?

"No, there was no one else. A long time ago, I had to hide in a rice field and stay quiet. I learned to know how many were around. He was by himself. He ran back toward the big pier."

57

Chuck goes to Church

He looked at all the leisure suits he had bought trying to decide which one would be appropriate for church. How would he know, he laughed? He had never been to church in his life. He laughed out loud as he thought the roof might fall in when he entered.

He had decided that day he counted the money what to do with the Reserve Notes of big denominations. He would put them in an envelope, visit Paul's church in Destin, sit through what he thought would be the dullest moments of his life, and he understood they collected what they called an offering. That was when he would put the envelope in the basket as he had seen it in a movie once.

He had written a note saying that in memory of Paul and his girlfriend, this money was to be used as the church decided. He knew he wasn't going to get any points with God, if there is one, but he thought the church could undoubtedly use the money.

Chuck had been shocked when he walked out onto the balcony, saw the crowd of people gathering down below the gazebo, and finally realized it was a funeral he was watching. He had no idea Paul and his girlfriend had been killed. He knew that Paul lived at the La Mancha for Paul had invited him to come see him and his mother once for dinner. He had refused, of course, because he also knew that Joe lived in the Dolphin building.

Chuck liked Paul. He respected him for doing the many things he did for his mother. During the few times they had talked together, he had learned of Paul's father's death and the unfortunate accident with the shark. He really respected the kid.

He secretly went to a football game one night when Paul had done so well before Paul had lost part of his left foot. He recognized the teacher sitting with the woman he guessed was Paul's mother. He had seen the old teacher at Tides Inn two or three times. He knew about Paul's good friend Doogs who meant so much to him.

He was certain no one had seen him standing way up there on the sixth floor, but he felt the sorrow and also the pride those people had for knowing Paul. He smiled, and that's when he decided to give Paul's church the money.

He had some trouble finding Faith Lutheran. He past it once and turned around in front of the YMCA and turned into the church. It was a beautiful building he thought as he followed a good-sized crowd into the lobby.

Because the fall weather had been so good, many tourists were still in the area, and he heard that several states nearby were having Fall Break, so the church was filling up. He was glad as that meant he wouldn't be noticed any more than many others, and whoever counted the collection money would have a hard time deciding a young bleach-blonde man had put the envelope in.

Chuck was surprised to find himself listening to the pastor and what he was saying. He knew his part of Launie's drug trafficking was wrong and that he should have run away a long time ago. He also knew that he had known no other life his entire life and that he had only Joe to trust in as he grew up.

They had been invited to take a Bible out of the rack in front of where they sat and as all the other people were doing it, Chuck reached up and got the Bible in front of him. He had never seen a Bible and as he sensed others were just turning to something called Hebrews, he had to look in the table of contents. There were so many names in the list the pastor was finished reading whatever it was before Chuck found the page. But as he sat listening, he convinced himself he had to find some really needy place to give the rest of the money. The lesson that day shocked him for it was about deeds, good deeds; not trying to set things right with God.

When the collection basket came to him he quickly put the envelope in never doubting that someone in the church would know what to do with the big bills. He hoped they found some collector who would pay lots of money for them.

He didn't wait around to greet the pastor at the end of the service as almost everyone was doing outside the lobby door under the porch where doughnuts and orange juice had been sit out on a table. He failed to see Trish Bishop standing in the little line waiting to say hello to Pastor Greg, but she saw him. She had seen him before she thought in a shiny red car at the La Mancha the week she had moved back to Destin but she guessed he was just a tourist visiting church. Chuck hurried to his car to head back to the La Mancha when he realized he was still holding the Bible. He tossed it in the back seat not wanting to go back inside. He wondered what the penalty for stealing from a church was, but who knew, he might just read some more.

When he arrived at Santa Rosa Blvd he turned right instead of going toward the La Mancha. He slowly guided the car down around the bend in the road until he was in front of Launie's with the Dorm behind it. Both places looked empty, but he realized it was Sunday. The racy green Cadillac was nowhere in sight, but he saw the Lollipop against a pier over in the Sound. As he drove away, he wondered if Launie would even recognize him if she were looking out a window.

An outrageous plan to spend the money entered his mind. He realized he could get arrested carrying out the plan, but if it worked, he would be helping a lot of young people. He almost ran a red light crossing Highway 98 as his mind was occupied. Going down the Blvd he passed his old penthouse and realized the key was still on his key ring. He wondered if he could get away with going up and getting his clothes, but he went on by saying to himself that he was starting a new life.

As he pull up to the guard house, he saw Marvin and the school teacher in the car in front of him. Marvin had stopped and they were talking with Gerald. He saw Gerald walk around to the passenger side and saw the teacher put his hand out the window. It was all wrapped up in bandages.

58
An Essay and a Football Game

School had been in session for almost a month now and students were anxiously waiting for Fall Break. Sometimes I read the Daily to catch the news about Doogs and the football team.

Morat spends more time walking around the La Mancha property and down on the beach than he does at City Hall and his boss, the Sheriff, is none too happy about it. I feel sympathetic toward Morat because I have no idea how Josephine Jones died. No one would doubt that Brantley had locked up his mother in the wardrobe, but no one could prove she was alive when he locked the door either. Morat's problem is how he's ever going to catch Brantley, even if Brantley did kill the dead girl Max found on the beach.

We are all being quiet about the matter as we don't want the tourists to think something is wrong at the La Mancha.

I was a little surprised when Doogs called one afternoon and asked if I would help him with a paper he had to write for Senior English. I hesitated, thinking of the hurt we both might have of seeing each other, but quickly said I would. He arrived and brought me a frozen fruit Popsicle which he knew I liked.

He looked at the scars where the arrow had entered and gone all the way through. He whistled and then in an almost sophomoric attitude exclaimed, "Wow, what a badge of honor, Prof!"

"Maybe you would like to find someone else to help you, I joked."

"No, I'll have to do with you."

They are reading Macbeth and are to write a paper using a line from the play which meant something to them personally.

Doogs looked sheepish as he pulled his paper from his backpack, "I'm not sure you will like this…"

"I have to read it first, don't I?"

He smiled and handed me the paper and went out on my balcony to sit until I was finished reading the paper.

He had chosen the most famous line of the play perhaps; MacBeth is giving up on the treacherous life he had lived as he says, "It is a tale told by an idiot, full of sound and fury, signifying nothing."

Doogs had started his paper with these words, "NO, not if you have a real friend…."

I could hardly read the paper as I had to keep blinking away tears as he wrote about how he and Paul had leaned on each other for the three and a half years they had known each other. He wrote with words which seemed to shout from the page that he was more than he could ever think to be because of his friend Paul. He ended it with, "I became a man, because he always was a man!"

I took two bottles of water from the refrigerator and carried them out to the balcony. I handed one to him.

He asked, "Was it silly to write that about a great Shakespearian play?"

"No, it was not. It was just what you needed to do. You understood just what to say."

"You know no one else will understand it."

"That's just fine. We do."

He gulped about half the bottle down, and almost choked. He was crying and got up and walked over to Paul's long board.

"I miss him so much…"

"I do too."

He surprised me as he said, "Will you come to this Friday's football game?"

I didn't think I would ever go to another game after Paul's death, but I too quickly said I would. I instantly dreaded for Friday to come.

Doogs called me again on Wednesday and told me Trish was going to the game also, and that she said she would stop and pick me up. After he hung up, I dreaded even more going for I hadn't seen Trish since she had moved back to Destin.

Fort Walton High had won all its games last year when Paul and Doogs shared playing quarterback.

Choctaw High, the other high school in Fort Walton Beach, had beat them soundly 34-14 in the third game this year. Every team member wanted to win this Friday. They wanted revenge. Doogs was the sole quarterback this year, and he was having a great season. Except for the one loss, they had won all their other games by a wide margin. Coaches from Georgia Tech wanted him to come to Atlanta next year, for he had statistics which were as good as any high school senior in the region.

Trish arrived to get me, and as we drove the few miles over to the packed parking lot at FWBH, we had little to say. We were both so nervous and thought we knew what the other one was thinking about—we were probably right.

On the second play of the game, Doogs threw a long pass to his wide receiver who caught it and took it in for the first score of the night. Trish and I were almost our old selves shouting and yelling until we were so hoarse we could hardly speak. The Vikings won the game easily, 56-0. Doogs had a tremendous game, passing for four touchdowns and running into the end zone for another. Long drives on the ground led to the other scores.

Choctaw seemed dumbfounded and made mistake after mistake. The Vikings revenge of the Warriors was sweet. I was amazed at the easy win, as was everyone around us.

As the final horn blew to signal the end of the game, Doogs picked up the ball and ran up into the stands where Trish and I were sitting. The whole student body of FWBH followed him across the field toward us. As he presented the ball to Trish, there was a tremendous cheer.

He looked at me and said, "It's for you too! He would like that."

When Trish let me out at my place, she pushed the football toward me.

I touched it and said, "No, that's yours. I have his board, you know."

She looked at me and gave a slight little sad smile. She and I agreed to get in touch with each other soon. Somehow, we never did.

59

You'll Burn Brantley

He had tried to get away from her by going to still another rig. He was hiding behind another wall of oil drums.

Suddenly one of them rolled away and she was standing there. He screamed.

"You pissed your pants, Brantley. You'll have to have a bath." He became the little boy who had been tormented and belittled by his mother so long.

He pulled the torn page of the Bible from his pants like he had done a bad thing. It took him a long time to get it out of his pocket for his finger was useless now; it was swollen so large it made his other fingers and thumb look tiny. Streaks of red ran all across the back of his hand and up his arm. He couldn't sleep became of the excruciating pain. He had not slept for two nights.

He cringed as she said, "For it is holy, Brantley! You'll get into real bad trouble for tearing the Bible, Brantley. You'll burn, Brantley."

She had underlined it many years ago and forced him to memorize it. Every time he did a 'wrong' thing, he had to say it to her and then go to the wardrobe.

His pants were a mess, but he didn't care. He looked down, tears filled his eyes and he could barely read what she had marked: John 15:6. Just the last part. 'he is thrown aside like a branch and he withers... he is gathered up and thrown into the fire, and he is burned....'" She had written 'Just for Brantley' at the top.

But he didn't need to read it for he knew it by heart. She had tormented him with the verse since he was being potty trained. He was terrified and trembled and cried when she had read it to him for he knew that then it was bath time.

The wardrobe flashed through his mind, the horrible closed-in place where no one could hear his screams. He felt the door pressing and holding him against the back of its insides. He felt himself falling on the floor at her knees when she finally opened it and let him out.

He swore to himself that he would never be taken to a place like that again.

He threw-up what little was inside him. The vomit splattered over the tops of his shoes and the deck of the rig.

60

Launie Buys Ollie a Treasure

Launie's compassion for Ollie was known by all the girls who lived in the Dorm. They were all dumbfounded that she showed so much concern for him and had little time for Chuck as some of them knew Chuck was Launie's real son.

Ollie's shooting rampage down the Blvd made the top headline in the Daily the day after it happened and was on the front page the rest of the week. It quoted Morat, "We cannot have someone like this loose in our community. We will not rest until we find this outlaw. The only clues we have is that the person was masked, may be a male or female and could be almost any age. We will search and question all residents of the Island to apprehend this dangerous fugitive."

Launie threw the paper in the floor in anger and fear. What if that State Trooper started snooping around her place? She wasn't worried much about that bungling clown Morat because he couldn't find his ass with both hands, but Blevins was smart.

She worked a plan over in her head.

The next morning she bought Ollie a classic More Fun Comic which introduces Oliver Queen as the Green Arrow from the comic store in Mary Ester. It cost her six hundred dollars as it was not in the best of condition; the store had another in much better shape but she had no intention of spending more to carry out her plan. She also inquired if her purchase could be returned and was told that it could if unopened from the plastic wrapper it was in.

Launie was caught in her emotions of caring for Ollie as she felt some responsibility for him and her fury at what he had done so close to her business on the Blvd. She had hidden him, she thought, with success for all these years and now he had made a spectacle of himself. She wondered how long it would be before someone came asking about him. Surely someone had recognized Ollie on the beach that day or on the Blvd when he acted like a maniac.

She blamed herself for what had happened because she was so concerned about finding the lost drug package and had exposed Ollie to the outside world. Launie seldom went inside the Library these days as she realized her appearance was not the sort of thing the johns would want to see. Besides, she had much more important business to take care of, but she had no doubt that locals were in the place every night—someone knew Ollie and would contact the police sooner or later.

She feared most though that beach kid who worked at the La Mancha. She had seen his classy little Fairlane too many times from her window in the Dorm and found out about him. La Mancha was the worse place on the whole damn Island for Ollie to have found the package, she thought—that idiot Morat was there all the time and that beach kid worked there. She knew she could not have anything like that happen again. All she needed was that State Trooper who was spending so much time in Fort Walton to come around asking questions.

Launie ordered two five gallon buckets of paint from Lowe's and had them delivered to the Dorm. When the salesman asked what color she wanted, she had replied she wanted sea foam green. There was much talk in the paint department at Lowe's about who in the world still used that color, but they had mixed it in the big plastic buckets and delivered it to her.

Launie knocked on Ollie's door two nights later. He seemed embarrassed and started straightening things up that were thrown around the room. Launie had never been in his rooms since he had moved in.

Ollie stammered, "I'm sorry about the mess Launie. No one ever comes to visit me."

"Don't worry about it, Ollie," she assured him. "I should be the sorry one for bothering you. I need you to help me carry some buckets of paint to the yacht and then go with me to Pensacola to help me there. Okay?"

Ollie had never been on the Lollipop but he admired it from his window as he could see it down at the little pier back of the Dorm. He fantasized that it was the boat Oliver Queen had fallen off before getting stranded on the island where he had to shoot his food with his arrows.

"That would be the trip of a lifetime, Launie! I would like that!

He grabbed one of the buckets and ran down the gravel path to the dock and ran back for the other one. Launie showed him where to place them.

He stepped onto the loading ramp and climbed the three steps up to the back deck. He looked around the expensive yacht and knew his billionaire hero would have been at home here. Ollie was smiling with a pride and happiness he had never experienced. Then, Launie gave him his real surprise.

He couldn't stand. He looked at it with amazement. He sat down at the little table at the back of the deck and turned the plastic package over and over.

"Is it really mine?"

"Yes, Ollie, you have earned it. I wanted you to have it."

"May I open it?"

"Why don't you wait until we get there?"

"Where are we going?"

"Down the Sound to Pensacola where I want you to help me paint the pier."

Launie knew that if someone were watching the Lollipop and she headed down the Sound they would not likely be followed. They would think she was taking the yacht to the slip at Pensacola.

She started the big boat and Ollie squealed with glee. He nearly danced as it pulled away from the pier. He glanced at where the drainage ditch emptied into the Sound and thought of his fort. He remembered how long it had taken him to cut all those words out of the *Daily*. He had cut-up three different copies before finding the words he wanted in really big type. He had started to say in the note that the first arrow in the sand was just him out having an adventure like his hero always does, but it would take too much trouble to find the words.

The dog on the chain behind one of the houses barked savagely at them as they passed, but Ollie laughed at it for he knew he was safe on the boat.

He yelled, "Shut-the-fuck-up! I'll shoot you like I did that barking bitch on the balcony," and he then gave it the finger as he has seen some of the girls do when they were disgusted.

Launie eased the Lollipop through the channel slowly as they passed the new jail. She could see people standing on the porch of the first floor above the dock for the patrol boats. She always had the fear that those boats would suddenly rush out and surround the yacht.

About another mile west of Fort Walton Beach, the Black Drainage Ditch deposits silt, debris, and sand into the dark waters of the Sound every time we have our heavy downpours. Once every five years or so, the Sound has to be dredged to keep the barge lane deep enough to navigate. Launie had seen the huge piles that had been scooped out on the bank from the dredging. She thought the water would be deep there.

When they arrived she maneuvered the boat out of the barge lane and to one side of the big deep hole. She stopped the Lollipop and turned on the lever that automatically dropped the anchor. She got the bottle of wine she had brought and two glasses and carried them to the table where Ollie now sat with the plastic bag in front of him.

"I thought we would stop here. Look, I brought the wine you like best!"

"Launie, you are so good to me. And my present! I love it!"

She poured the wine, sat his on the little table as she stepped around behind him, "Why don't you open it now? I'll watch you turn the pages from here over your shoulder. No, wait, let's drink the wine first."

He was so excited that his had trembled as he picked up the glass and started to turn to her.

"No, don't turn around Ollie, look at the package. I want you to see it and I want to feel your happiness."

As he lifted his glass to drink, she pulled the little plated revolver from her skirt pocket. He took a big drink of the wine and put the glass back on the table as he reached for the comic. Her hand trembled for just a second, and shot him at the base of his skull. He shrugged, collapsed on the table, and a little blood starting running across the plastic package.

Launie became the raving bitch that Chuck knew so well when she was angry or frightened. She snatched the package and as she pulled it away his hand smeared the blood across it leaving the imprint of his fingers.

She had the handcuffs she had used in her raunchiest days. She put one around each of his wrists, dragged the buckets of paint one by one up to him and put a cuff around each bail. Sweat ran down her bare sides inside her blouse by the time she pushed him over the back of the boat. She stood, took a deep breath, walked over to the table where her glass of wine still sat undisturbed, raised it to her mouth and drank it in one gulp.

Launie hadn't seen the young couple lying on a blanket on the high north bank of the Sound. Sam Ripley a military Med Corpsman at Eglin, had taken his fiancée Alice there many times since he had been stationed at Elgin. They had hurried to conceal themselves when they heard the Lollipop approaching because both of them were nearly naked. They peeked over the edge of the bank where they were lying and in the light from the deck lamp of the yacht had seen the murder as it happened. Alice had cried out just as the shot went off but Launie had not heard her.

Sam held his hand over her mouth as they watched the killer pull the body and heard the splash as it hit the dark water. They saw her collapse in a chair at the little table and drain her glass in one drink and then take a paper from her pocket, raise it to her nose and sniff at it violently. Sam knew what that meant.

Launie would have seen the glow from Sam's cell phone if she had looked back as he was alerting the Security Office on base about the murder before the lights of the Lollipop disappeared into the darkness.

Twenty or so minutes later as Launie steered the yacht slowly past the jail and toward the dock behind the Dorm, she heard the wail of sirens as several police cars raced east through Fort Walton and over Brooks Bridge. She wasn't concerned because it wasn't unusual for that to happen out on 98. She had just anchored the yacht and headed up toward the Dorm when she realized all the cars had turned down the street toward her.

Heavily armed men piled out of the cars and headed toward her. She whirled around and stumbled back toward the Lollipop and saw the flashing lights of two Okaloosa County Patrol Boats blocking the dock.

She stood there on the gravel path shaking uncontrollably.

61

Barren Ground

"They're empty. All of them."

Attorney Matt Schaberg had arrived from Miami ten days earlier. During their first meeting, Launie had told him of the safe deposit boxes in the banks, she told him the keys were in a little box at the Dorm, but he had refused to go there. From the jail's own notary, Launie had signed a letter giving him power-of-attorney to open the boxes. He had made the rounds to each only to find that all the boxes were empty. In one of them, he found a note.

He handed it to Launie across the conference table where they sat. She opened it and read, "No doubt you will succeed in getting all these boxes filled up again, but I'm taking this to do some good somewhere." It was signed, 'Chuck.'

"That thieving son-of-a-bitch."

Even on a callous lawyer like Schaberg, the irony of what she had just said was not lost.

"They told me to get on a plane and return if you couldn't afford my fees."

"You can't leave me now. I have nothing..."

"You know the arrangements. Miss Sanderson, you have trouble listening to people. They told you long ago to get rid of that yacht that attracts so much attention. Remember, they suggested a fishing boat? They told you to quit sending your girls all around to do things, like buy food at Tides Inn or deliver whatever it is you take to the La Mancha twice a month. They said you know what you have to do too.

And…they said something about someone being in the courtroom if this ever went to trial. Someone who has nothing to lose. Someone whose family will be well taken care of."

Maybe for the first time in her life Launie was really afraid. She started to plead and as she looked into Schaberg's eyes, she saw he really didn't give a damn. She started to cry, really cry—not Launie cry, but scared crying.

Schaberg pulled his handkerchief from his pocket and handed it to Launie. The guard watching through the window jerked the door open and announced the conversation was over.

"I wish you the best," he said as he picked up his brief case, went to the door and exited. He could hear Launie screaming obscenities through the heavy metal door after it closed behind him.

The jail is in the shape of a Celtic cross if you looked down from the sky. The first floor houses male prisoners and has the admitting office and conference rooms, the second has the offices of the sheriff and his help, and the third floor has the cafeteria and cells for the women, and the one wing extends out over the Sound making it easy access for the water patrol boats to dock underneath.

As the elevator took them to the third floor, Launie looked at the tiny pill in her palm. She spewed out a string of obscenities and licked her palm. She didn't realize the pill had dropped from her hand and had fallen into the crack between the elevator doors and fallen into the shaft below. She knew what the pill would do and that it probably wouldn't be traceable for her death would seem to be a heart attack.

The elevator opened onto the third floor and as the guard stepped into the hall, Launie raised both arms above her head and hit the guard with all her force. The sound of the cuffs hitting her head just before the woman hit the floor with a thud could be heard way down the hall. Launie bolted toward where the four halls intersected. When she reached there, she turned down one of them and ran as fast as her enormous weight would let her.

During the three weeks she had been in jail, she hadn't had any drugs at all. She had cried and begged the first week, but finally had sobered up. Now her head was aching and she couldn't think straight. She felt she was fainting as she lumbered down the hall toward the big window at the end. She knew it overlooked the water and that she would rather drown than bear the pain she knew was coming. She crashed through the window with three or four guards closing in on her.

Launie had turned the wrong direction at the intersection of the halls. She screamed one time as she fell through the air as she had time to see the pilings and the dirt that had been pounded down so the basement could be poured at the construction site for an addition to the jail.

She hit the hard barren ground. The guards looking through the broken window above saw the dark, almost black stain of the blood as it began to puddle around her head.

62

A New Tombstone

Libby Morat visited Memorial Cemetery on a regular basis to put flowers on Josephine's grave and to sit on the bench nearby and wonder about all the tragedies of the summer. She found the cemetery peaceful and a place where she could escape from the whirlwind of troubles at the La Mancha.

When she arrived about a week later, she passed a new grave. Libby sat on the bench by Josephine's grave as two taxies pulled into the gate of the cemetery. A group of women got out and stood in a semi-circle around the new grave. One by one they placed something on the ground in front of the new tombstone.

When they left, they got into two taxies that had many pieces of luggage and boxes strapped to the racks on their tops.

Curiosity caused Libby to walk over to the new tombstone where she read 'Ollie.' There was nothing else on the stone except a chiseled arrow underneath the name.

She was a little surprised to see a neat circle of crushed beer cans—crushed into little flat medallions, laying up close to the stone.

She looked up at the disappearing taxis and saw that J C Blevins was following close behind them.

But she had found the biggest mystery at Josephine's grave because by the stone she and Emile and the Prof had erected stood a new stone. It said, 'Joe Kroeger – Big Brother.'

Libby sat on the bench. New mysteries filled her mind.

Who had the stone erected? Joe Kroeger? What did it mean 'Big Brother?'

63

Fire

He saw the shape of his mother sitting beside him in the cockpit. She turned toward him and looked in his eyes, "Take us home now... Take us now... Mind me!" He had never refused her orders except that one time, and often wished he had the guts to do so, but as she ordered he turned the copter away from the rig where he thought he would be safe and flew out into the Gulf. He pulled back on the throttle and the copter sped out toward the north.

When it was about a hundred miles straight to the beach at the La Mancha, his mother never stopped saying over and over to him, "Take us home now." Brantley's hand gripped the arm of his seat and he screamed. Finally he saw the familiar lights of the La Mancha with every building lit up as a protection of getting hit by a plane in the night. It was welcoming him home.

Brantley thought of the verse. The shock of what he thought next caused him to shake uncontrollably; she wanted him to crash into their building. She wanted him to go up in a ball of fire. She was still trying to control him. He had to resist, but except for that spur of the moment when he shoved her into the wardrobe, he never had.

Brantley smiled and rocked back and forth trying to get the copter to go faster. He was in control. He turned and glared at her there beside him, and he bellowed the worst thing he could think of, "Piss on you! Just piss on you!"

Suddenly another plane flying out of the Air Command had turned on its powerful search light. Brantley nearly lost control of the Sikorsky as he was terrified all at once of being caught. This fear was greater than all the others; he would not go back into a closed-in space. He turned to yell at his mother, but she had disappeared from the seat next to him, and he cried for her help.

She had left him again. Again when he needed her most...

He turned the copter and it banked toward the right on a more direct route to the La Mancha. The other copter's lights looked much closer to him and now they were turned toward him. Brantley lost control of what was left of his reason. He screamed for the other copter to get out of his way. He damned it to crash into the dark water below him. He would not go back into her cell... He would not go into any cell...

He suddenly knew what he had to do as he pushed forward on the control and the Sikorsky fell toward the water. Its lights lit up a wide circle in the water even though he was at more than five hundred feet. He would skim over the top of the gazebo and pool house, fly straight at the two buildings behind the pool, pull up, and barely missed the roofs and swooped around and head back out over the Gulf. He knew how everything was situated and doubted the other pilot could pull off the same maneuver.

The Search and Rescue copter with Marvin and the pilot had made it out toward Brantley's copter much farther than they thought they could before they were forced to turn on their search beam. When the other copter had suddenly appeared to fall from the sky, they had turned to follow it into shore.

"God, Almighty!" Marvin yelled as they saw Brantley's Sikorsky hit the roof of the gazebo, snap off the tops of three palm trees between there and the big pool, and slam into the pool fence and flop over top down into the deep end.

I, too, saw the whole disaster as I was in my usual place at that time of night, on my balcony. I watched in amazement and then horror as the helicopter came toward the gazebo and slammed into the pool. Suddenly I saw a line of flames streak across the pool deck from the outdoor bar-b-q where some young people had been cooking out earlier that evening.

The explosion echoed far across the water; it sounded like a bomb from a war. The water and the circle of buildings caused the explosion to be much louder than it actually was. The heat was fierce on my face and arms. A thought ran through my mind how thankful we should all be that it was after 11 p.m. and the pool was empty and closed.

The fuel tank must have been almost full as a great ball of flame rose in the air and the sound of the blast reverberated out across the water magnifying as it went, and rocked the windows in the buildings. I could hear the sizzle of hot metals as they fell back into pool. I could see fire on the water around where the copter had been as the oil burned. One of the skid shoes of the copter broke loose and was hurled past the yellow police tape sliding down the sidewalk and coming to rest in front of the sliding glass doors of a condo.

Lights from many condos in the Pelican and the Dolphin came on seconds later, and soon many people stood on their balconies looking down at the balls of fire as they seemed to skip across the pool. The boardwalk was ablaze and the gazebo was nearly gone. Chunks of the pool wall were thrown into the pool on top of the upside down Sikorsky.

The Search and Rescue helicopter hovered over what was left of the gazebo. Sirens started sounding as fire trucks, three or four of them, rushed down the Blvd toward us.

The emergency sirens—the big ones that blare out and can be heard for miles when a storm or some other disaster is approaching started wailing. I saw several boats speeding out from Anglers Pier heading out, I imagine, to see if help was needed. Several aircraft flew out of Eglin, circled and turned back. The Search and Rescue pilot must have told them what had happened.

The ball of fire had blasted into the night sky and waves reflected it way out toward the horizon. The stench of fuel and the burning kept coming at us for minutes.

64

Can't Say Goodbye

Paul's tragic accident-filled life came to an all too soon ending. I sit on my balcony and sorrow and hurt fills me like none I have felt for a long time. Through approaching tears, I imagine a tall straight Huck who will never again be silhouetted against the horizon by the setting sun. But then I remember he will always be a part of the water he loved so much. I think of Doogs's paper and deny Mr. Shakespeare with all my heart, because Paul's life gave pleasure to many.

I look at the spot where he used to sit and watch Jonathan L, and it came to me that Paul was just like that seagull; he flew on his own and made his own way. He was a man worth knowing. His paddle board and paddle sit leaning against a wall on my balcony; sometimes I can't bear to look at them, but I'll never get rid of them for I can't rid myself of him.

Sometimes at night I go down and sit on that place on the wall. I have planted a sea oat right in front of the spot. I look out and he appears in my mind silhouetted against the setting sun riding straight and tall. And sometimes, I really do see a gull soaring high up in the sky.

The Air Patrol still flies over with a speed and gracefulness I am always amazed about, and if I'm lucky they fly by twice. They fly in perfect V formation sometimes, but occasionally there is a vacant spot in the formation as if one of them died. I wonder, do they feel a hurt and a vacant place like I do?

I don't walk as far as I did earlier in the summer. There are too many memories down there that will probably haunt me during the few years I have left, but if I've timed it just right as I turn to head back east, the sun is making its appearance for a new day. If I'm lucky, the clouds will be tinged with gold.

Skipper isn't allowed on the beach with me, but as I climb back up to the gazebo, I always see him with his lop-sided head poking through the railing of my balcony. His familiar bark fills the morning air as he wiggles all over waiting for me to get up to the condo and feed him his breakfast. I still put the collar on him that Josephine Jones bought for him—the one with the blue stones circling it—whenever we go walking.

Epilogue

Launie's Gentlemen's Library was closed, of course. The *NorthWest Daily* quoted Blevins. He said he found the strangest thing when he went through The Dorm. All the rooms were in good order, that it looked like people had left in a hurry, but when he came to the big bedroom in the back, there were broken liquor bottles on the floor and the ornate purple headboard had been slid apart at the middle and the concealed safe behind it was wide open and empty.

Elsewhere in the *Daily* under *Unusual News,* a ticket agent for United told about two taxies arriving with ten young women and many pieces of luggage. The strange thing was they had all paid for their tickets with cash, large domination bills.

Blevins had followed the two taxies from the Dorm to the cemetery and on to the airport. He had no way of stopping the girls for there was no reason to suspect them of any of Launie's doings, but he did find out where they were going and had pictures of each of them.

When the guards got down to Launie after she made the suicide jump through the jail window, they saw her hands clawing at the packed soil and she was rushed to Sacred Heart Hospital where she spent the winter recuperating from several broken bones, a collapsed lung, and other internal injuries. She is back in jail, I hear, and is awaiting a Grand Jury's decision about charges against her. Like everyone else in town all I know is what Prosecuting Attorney Curt Porter is reporting in the Daily news.

The day I read that notice in the *Daily,* I received another photo card with the same handwriting as the first one. Written across the front was, "No greater love can a man have, than to give his life for others." It was a picture taken somewhere in a rough part of a big city under a raised rail line; a long line of people, homeless people it appeared, were waiting their turns to go into the storefront building that had a sign in the window, 'Come, eat!' I don't know who is sending the cards and taking care of so many, but maybe I'll figure it out.

When Marvin came to say goodbye, he smiled as I told him about the cards and money.

"You know who's doing it. He's trying to atone for what they did."

"You know, my good friend, that in the worst tragedies ever written or lived, innocent people have been caught up in the scheme of things and sometimes those innocent ones become heroes if they can escape. I hope he's getting a peacefulness and joy from doing it."

"And you are right, my good friend, sometimes they just need a little push by someone in the right direction. I will come back and see you, and find out the next chapter."

We gave each other a man hug and I told him I hoped he would.

They found Launie's Cadillac in a parking lot in Pensacola. Police impounded it as Morat had convinced them he needed it swept for blood and DNA. They only thing they found was a picture behind the sun visor on the driver's side of Launie when she was much younger sitting on a levee in New Orleans with two little boys. Morat thought the boys looked familiar, but he couldn't connect it all in his mind. Of course, I knew who drove it all the time it was on the Island—Chuck.

Brantley's condo sits empty as if even the tourists know its history. They buried his mother's body in the cemetery which overlooks the Sound. I think of Brantley often as I can picture him going around the grounds picking up everyone's trash. I remember the article about his service to the company he flew the copter for and the praise they had for him. I remember the letters from the grateful children to him for saving their fathers and the appreciation he had of hanging them over his seat in the one thing he controlled in his life, his Sikorsky.

Brantley had to live in two worlds which finally scrambled his mind and the controlling world got the better of him. Perhaps Brantley escaped in the only way he could control. Brantley was a murderer and had to pay for what he had done, but maybe, just maybe if someone had helped him earlier, that wouldn't have happened.

After all the tension and heart burns he had suffered at the La Mancha, it was a surprise when Morat and his wife Libby bought a condo over in Sea Turtle building. I see him almost every day as he sits on a bench on the west boardwalk looking out at the Gulf.

Trish could not stand to live in the condo at the La Mancha and decided to move away. Since Paul's death, we seldom saw her out and around the property. I would go and knock on the door only to be told from behind the closed door that she was okay, or to walk away without her answering my knock.

The day she left to move back to Destin, she called me and asked me to come over. I hurried to her condo and when she opened the door, she handed me the copy of Jonathan Livingston Seagull. She leaned toward me, kissed me on the cheek, and closed the door. Paul had written on the title page: 'From the best friend (besides Doogs) I have ever had.'

At the City Council meeting this week, the clerk announced that an anonymous benefactor had given Fort Walton Beach $3,000,000 to finish the state of the art technological center for the young people of the city. Ironically, it's being construction on the land where Launie's Gentlemen's Library and The Dorm had stood before they mysteriously burned. The Daily has been trying since to discover who the benefactor is, but I have a feeling they never will. The center will be named in honor of Paul.

The destruction of the gazebo, the east boardwalk, and the pool created about as much havoc at the La Mancha as the murder investigation had. Marvin was gone and we have a new man in charge of buildings and grounds—Craig. He's much like Marvin, a man who tells it like it is. Somehow, I bet he's not the man Marvin is.

Max got fired because he hadn't told Security or the police who Ollie was. Max is still a beach bum somewhere, I imagine. I heard he is trying to get his Life Saver certificate and I read in the Daily that he won a diving event in Sea Side the other day. He's one of those good-looking guys who sometimes marries into a fortune or sometimes marries into a nightmare. I hope his love for women takes him neither place, but to just happiness.

We didn't have too many visitors the rest of the summer as many canceled their reservations when they learned that nearly the whole beach front was a clean-up and construction site. Outside contractors had to be brought in and it took months to get most things working again.

Doogs wised-up and is at Gainesville. He's in pre-med classes and texts me about twice a week for me to review and correct grammar on some paper he emails me. He had told me when I handed him the bank statement in his name that the only way he could afford college was his football scholarship, and that the money in the account would get him through medical school.

He keeps thanking me for the money although I have told him many times that I received a photo card one day with the name of a bank and a series of numbers on it. The card had a picture of a shiny red car in the background. When I finally figured out what the numbers meant, I had gone to the bank and found an account with over a million dollars in it. The card had said, "See that Doogs gets through school." He asked me several times who it was, and I told him the truth each time, "I really don't know."

He's on the football team, but like many high school stars, he doesn't play quarterback. He told me last week, he's met a nice girl named Jeanne. Who knows what will happen there.

One afternoon in late fall my cell phone rang and as I looked at it I saw it was a local number I didn't recognized. I answered it and Ryan apologized for bothering me. I told him to quit apologizing and that I was indeed glad to hear from him.

He wanted to know if he could take me to dinner. I told him that he could come to my condo for dinner. I started to tell him how to get to it, but he said that he knew where it was because he and Paul had sat on the wall beneath my balcony one afternoon. We made arrangements to eat together two nights later.

When he arrived like everyone else who had been to see me, he had to see the scars. I think I would have hit him had he said anything like Doogs had, but he was very concerned and ask if we had any idea who had done it and why.

I told him Blevins and everyone else was stumped with the whole incident.

I had some pretty good rib steaks that I grilled on my little electric grill on the balcony. Ryan ate like he hadn't eaten for days, and when his plate was clean, he sheepishly said, "Guess you think I was hungry? Well, I was. I'm not a very good cook and I hate eating out."

I said, "Half my steak is still here on my plate, and you're welcome to eat if you want to eat it after I've cut on it."

He said, "Sure," and reached over and jabbed the steak with his fork.

I smiled.

229

After we ate, we sat on the balcony like Paul and I used to and Ryan told me that Paul and he were so much alike in so many ways. He talked about Paul's love of the Gulf and his own love of what was in the Gulf.

I asked, Why aren't you following that dream and finding out?"

He shrugged and looked embarrassed, "Money and I've been out of school so long. I don't know if I could cut it."

"I don't believe you would have any trouble with the last part because I have heard about you. Marvin said when you make up your mind to do something, it gets done."

Then I told him about the money that had mysteriously appeared, and said there was plenty for him.

"I couldn't take your money!"

"It sure isn't mine; I'm a retired teacher you know. No, someone had all this money and wanted to help others. I think I am just in the right spot so someone thinks I would use it and be fair with it. I have an idea who it might be but I'm not sure. I also have an idea that the money might have come from a place it shouldn't have, but as the bank manager said, we have no way of proving anything."

I saw a look of hurt fill his eyes and was a little surprised at what he said next.

"You know, I miss Brantley too. It's sorta the same—I just happened to be there and he needed me and I needed him. He sure made me work harder in class. I stayed out of trouble at home because my grades improved so much; I used him. I didn't even know his last name. I never asked about his father. I never went to his house in the whole three years we knew each other in school. I don't know what his mother's name was. I knew there were problems between them. She was always waiting for him after school or practice. She always pulled up in front of my house when she would let Brantley come eat with us and honk the horn... I wish I have done a better job of being a friend to him."

"We can't help those that close us off, and Brantley had a reason for doing that that we will never know. Now, do you want to go to college?"

He looked embarrassed again and said sort of awkwardly, "Sure, I want to go to school. I work hard and try to save and something always comes along and costs me what I have saved. I'm not prepared for much of anything and I only have full-time work in the summer. I just can't seem to get it together. And my mom sure can't help."

"Then take some of the money and do what you dream to do!"

"Do I hug you now, or something?"

"Coach Brown said you might just say that."

He laughed and turned away with his face bright red. He saw Paul's board standing against the wall and asked if he might borrow it sometime?

I said I would be happy about that and I knew Paul would too.

We discussed what he wanted to do about school and I got a big surprise.

"Ichthyology."

"You sure?"

"Yep, wanted to know what's under those waves out there for as long as I've seen it. Marine Biology is next if I can."

"Oh, you can. We'll see to it!"

He's in Gainesville too as he was accepted in January to study Ichthyology. He's scared about being out of school so long, but I promised to help as much as I could and he's glad Doogs is there.

Marvin was right that day at the pool when he said Ryan Tilley was just as good a man as Paul Bishop.

*

The dolphins love the point in front of the La Mancha where the fishing always has been good. They remind me of horses on a merry-go-round as they leap in and out of the water. Yesterday morning when I walked, I saw three baby ones in the pod as they trolled back and forth for fish.

Jonathan L sits on the volleyball goal post, or maybe it's not him but his offspring. All his relatives and friends still fill the air and beach with their shrieks and fights (swine birds). But often I see him take off and fly way up high outlined in the beautiful sunset that fills our skies.

The waves either crash into the shore with a show of the great power of the Gulf, or they hardly touch the Island at all with a gentleness that is very calming; always changing, always mysterious…

About the Author

The author moved to the Panhandle of Florida after teaching literature for many years in Albuquerque. He has traveled to Europe several times and much of the United States where his knowledge and admiration of other cultures grew and these characteristics are apparent in his writings. He is an avid people watcher, much like the Prof of the novel, and uses unusual traits to round out his people in his writing. His love of writing and traveling are exceeded only by his love for his five grandchildren.

Printed in the United States
By Bookmasters